Debt Collector

HARD TO KILL

JON MILLS

DIRECT RESPONSE PUBLISHING

ISBN-13: 978-1534874114
ISBN-10: 1534874119

Also By Jon Mills

Undisclosed
Retribution
Clandestine
The Debt Collector
Debt Collector: Vengeance
Debt Collector: Reborn
Debt Collector: Hard to Kill
Debt Collector: Angel of Death
Debt Collector: Prey
Debt Collector: Narc
Debt Collector: Hard Time
Debt Collector: Her Last Breath
Debt Collector: Trail of the Zodiac
Debt Collector: Fight Game
The Promise
True Connection
Lost Girls
I'm Still Here

Dedication

For my family.

Chapter 1

NEW ORLEANS

PRESENT DAY

Out of all the bars in New Orleans, they had to pick the one he was in. When the guy snapped the pool cue in half, Jack cursed under his breath and prepared for the worst.

Ten minutes prior, he'd been casually sitting at the bar sipping on bourbon thinking about the conversation he'd had with his ex, Theresa. She was holding down a job as a waitress at a fancy cocktail bar in the French Quarter. He'd been in New Orleans for just under a month and it had taken him the better part of two weeks to summon the nerve to go speak to her. It wasn't that they had finished on bad terms or that he didn't think she would give him the time of day, but they hadn't seen each other in over eight years. Four of those he'd been inside and well, after the trouble in L.A., he had gone back and forth on whether to check in on her.

The look on her face when she came over to get his order was priceless.

Now, it was late evening and Bourbon Street was crowded with drunk tourists. He had managed to find a small, low-key place down on Frenchmen Street, about ten minutes from her workplace.

He wasn't looking to get plastered, just have a few drinks, maybe find some company and return to his room at the Hotel Royal. What should have been a quiet evening turned into chaos after five guys came into the joint. For the first half an hour he didn't pay much attention to them. They ordered pitchers and tucked themselves away in the far corner of the room where the pool tables were. The bar was dimly lit, six booths off to the side and a small dance floor that wasn't currently in use. There was a rowdy bunch of tourists eating oysters and drinking beer just down from him. He'd just wanted to be alone with his thoughts but Murphy's Law said otherwise.

Over the span of an hour the place soon filled up with patrons until folks were shoulder to shoulder. He cursed under his breath at the guy who had referred him to the place. *It's quiet. No trouble, he said.* A mass of sweaty bodies mingled, people chatted and glasses clinked. Perhaps the evening might have ended well if it wasn't for a rabble of girls who came in just after nine. From the moment they stepped in the door, eyes were on them and they knew it. They wore skimpy cut-off shorts, loose tops that showed off their cleavage and they looked as if they were on the prowl for a good time. Out the corner of his eye, Jack watched as they ordered shots and starting dancing all provocatively. One of them took a selfie while another pretended to put her tongue in her friend's ear. The beat of the music was low until one of them asked the bartender to turn it up. The bartender tossed them a nonchalant look and reached under the bar. The volume went up a few notches and the dark-haired girl with large brown eyes looked pleased. She shot Jack a seductive glance before twirling out onto the dance floor to join her other friends.

Jack swiveled on his stool, rested his elbows on the bar and admired the view. It had been a while since he'd been with a woman. In the back of his mind he had kind of hoped that his ex was single but she wasn't. Theresa made it clear that she had a guy, a good one and she wasn't interested in picking back up where they had left off. The conversation that day lasted no more than five minutes.

"Now that's trouble if I've ever seen it."

Jack cast a glance over his shoulder. The bartender was wiping down the counter. He was college age, probably trying to make some dough to get through whatever he was majoring in by day. When Jack looked back, three of the five guys had ambled out onto the dance floor and managed to edge their way in among the women. The other two were still playing pool but occasionally glancing over and smirking. At first it looked as if the ladies were into it. A couple of the women ground up against the guys and ran their hands through their hair. It was your typical flirting that was to be found in a bar when folks got tanked up on liquor. However, it was the one who'd asked for the music to be turned up that caught his attention. A large black fella was pulling her into him even though she appeared to be telling him to let her go.

"Hey!" the bartender yelled over. "Give the lady some space."

The guy sneered and broke into laughter backing away and joining his other two friends at the pool table. His two buddies didn't seem to be having any trouble with the other girls. They continued dancing away completely oblivious to their pal's misfortune.

The girl came over to the bar looking red-faced and pissed. She fished around inside her purse and applied a fresh coat of lipstick. Jack didn't look directly at her. He continued sipping on his drink while she placed an order.

"Thanks, Matt," the girl said to the bartender. "The guy's an asshole."

"They usually are," the bartender muttered.

Out the corner of her eye Jack saw her glance at him while Matt placed a cold bottle of beer in front of her.

"Waiting for someone?"

At first he didn't think she was speaking to him.

"Me? No."

"I'm Rachael."

Jack cast a glance at her and nodded. She couldn't have been more than twenty-five. Pretty. The kind of girl he could quite easily have slipped into bed with back in New York. Back then he didn't care how old they were as long as they were over twenty-five, though even that that was a little on the young side for him. Most of the women he'd met were in their early thirties, but occasionally a few would slide in looking older than they were.

"Jack," he replied.

He watched her friends dancing.

"I didn't want to come out tonight but," she gave a nod to her friends, "they dragged me out. Said it would be good for me. You know, after breaking up with my boyfriend." She emphasized the word boyfriend. "To be honest I'm just not into the bar scene. What about you?"

"Depends on the crowd."

He let her talk. His mind was still preoccupied with Theresa.

"So, you from New Orleans or visiting?"

"Just passing through."

She nodded before taking a swig of her drink. "On vacation?"

"Something like that."

His eyes drifted from the dance floor over to the pool area. The black dude muttered something into his friend's ear before ambling over. Obviously, "no" meant very little to him. It wasn't uncommon to see a guy try a second time. It all depended on the woman. Those who knew their worth would shut them down again, others might see their persistence as endearing. It took all types.

Rachael was still talking to Jack when the guy came up alongside her.

"Hey, I think we got off to a bad start. How about I

buy you a drink?"

She held up her bottle. "Already have one." She looked back at Jack. The guy looked Jack over before trying again.

"C'mon, loosen up a little. Your friends seem to be doing fine."

"Look, I'm not interested," she said.

Some might have thought that would have been the moment to walk away with your dignity in check, but not this fool. No, the alcohol had blocked out what little computing power he had in his tiny brain.

She snorted.

"Whore," he muttered as he turned to leave.

"What the hell did you call me?"

Now she had every right to go off on him but this was only going to end badly.

"You heard."

She grasped a handful of his shirt and shoved him He turned and grabbed a hold of her arm. Jack sighed. This was not going to be the peaceful night he envisioned.

Jack turned to him and spoke in a calm voice. "Let her go."

"Stay out of this, man."

"Get off my arm," she said again struggling to free herself.

"Not until you come over and have that drink with me. I know what you girls are like. Coming in here flaunting it all over the place."

"Let go of me." She tugged hard but he only seemed to enjoy it.

Jack slipped off the stool, whacked back the remainder of his drink and placed the glass on the counter.

"You should listen to her."

He sneered. "What? What are you going to do?"

Back in his early days he would have pulled the guy outside and beat him within an inch of his life, now, with the FBI probably looking for him, avoidance was a must. Thankfully he didn't have to say any more as Matt from behind the bar reappeared.

"If you guys are going to start trouble, take it out,

before I call the cops."

The guy didn't even reply to the bartender; he was too busy eyeballing Jack. Jack glared back at him and for once, it was kind of nice not to throw a punch or bend a guy's arm around. The hulking fella released his grip and backed away. "Whatever."

"Jerk!" the girl said looking red in the face.

The asshole walked back over to his buddies.

"Thank you," she said before going into some rant about how guys didn't have manners. Jack wasn't paying any attention to her. He was still watching the guy as he returned to the table, took another swig of his drink and said something to his pal. They looked as if they were trying to tell him that it wasn't worth it. It didn't work. A minute later he picked up a cue stick and snapped it in half.

Shit, Jack thought. *There's always one.*

What frame of mind did you have to be in to want to take things that far? The frame of mind that came from being filled up with liquid courage. His two buddies followed for moral support while the others on the dance floor were too busy with Rachael's friends to notice.

Now every guy was different. You had the ones who were full of themselves but unsure of their own ability — they were all mouth and no action. Then there were the ones who were ready to fight but they really had to have their buttons jabbed to push them over the edge. Those he didn't have to worry about. It was the psychos. The ones who didn't think at all, instead they reacted. This guy was one of those. He wasn't into theatrics like some of the punks he'd met along his travels.

Jack saw the pool cue coming at him out the corner of his eye. He slid back fast, grabbed the guy's wrist, and gave him a right hook into the side of his face before he could wheel the other half up.

That was all it took for his four buddies to step up to the plate. He didn't wait for them to charge him before he grabbed her bottle of beer and tossed it at the head of the first guy. It hit him square on the nose sending him down with blood gushing out. The second guy caught him in the side with a punch. Jack parried his blow with an elbow in the gut and an uppercut to the face. The two guys on the dance floor attacked him at the same time, throwing him back against the bar while the large black guy got back up and reached for the snapped pool cue. He didn't get close enough to use it though. Jack gave him a swift kick to the nuts and then slammed his head into the nose of the guy to his left that was holding his arm. The other one let him go and made a run for it. There was always one who ran. Loyalty only went so far.

As the men groaned and writhed around on the floor, Rachael turned to him.

"You want to get out of here?"

He smirked. There it was, the opportunity to end the night on a good note. The thought of taking her back and spending the next hour tangled up under the sheets sounded good but after the day he'd had, he just wanted to be left alone.

"As much as I would love to, and don't take this wrong way, as you are..." he sucked air between his teeth.

"I'm just going to call it a night."

With that said, Jack turned, fished a few dollars out of his pocket and tossed it on the counter. Matt gave him a curt nod. As he walked back out onto the busy streets, he didn't realize that his presence in New Orleans had set in motion a chain of events that would come back to bite him in the ass. Nevertheless, he'd soon find out.

Chapter 2

Sicily, Italy

Salvatore Nicchi sat at a small café table overlooking the turquoise Mediterranean. Behind him a bustling marketplace, colorful street life, and the ancient ruins of Palermo. He sipped on his small espresso. His mind was lost in the past. So many years had flown by since his rise to power with his brother Vito. He recalled being seventeen. Both of them having a head full of dreams, and never really realizing the cost of living a life inside organized crime.

Now Vito was dead.

It wasn't that he expected his brother to live long into his seventies. He knew what he was like. His need to teach people a lesson had put him in the crosshairs of more than one hit man. Hell, some were hired by the same organization.

But it was still his brother. His flesh and blood. Some

things superseded the organization.

They had buried more than enough family members.

"More coffee, sir?"

"Thank you."

Unlike Vito he had let others take on the risky jobs. Salvatore remained behind the curtain, pulling the strings and guiding the affairs of Cosa Nostra the way his father and grandfather before him had done. It was the reason they had lived long into their nineties. They got to see their children grow without the fear of being killed. He intended to do the same.

Salvatore basked in the sun-drenched hills that surrounded the capital with an ache in his heart. If only Vito had listened to him. He should have been here, by his side, enjoying the wealth they had obtained. But that wasn't meant to be.

The waiter topped up his cup from a French press. A small amount dripped onto the white tablecloth.

"My apologies, sir. I will get a new one."

Salvatore waved him off. "It's okay, Alberto."

He returned to looking out at the glassy blue sea as sixty-foot schooners bobbed along, and fishermen brought in their nets. He breathed in the salty, warm air while closing his eyes and remembering better days.

Time seemed to stand still as he wandered through the memories.

Even when he heard a chair across from him being pulled out he didn't open his eyes.

"Good day, Giovanni," he said softly.

The aroma of his thin cigar reached his nostrils before he met his gaze.

"It's been a long time."

"That it has."

"How is business?"

"I can't complain."

"Your mother?"

"She is well. She passes on her thanks."

Giovanni gestured to the waiter and asked him to bring him some coffee. Giovanni was a man who dressed impeccably. He wore only the finest suits, tailored to his huge frame. That morning he was dressed in a tight, black suit, white shirt and red tie. Salvatore's introduction to him was unlike any other. His mind drifted back to a day he would never forget. Giovanni had been paid handsomely to assassinate Salvatore by a rival member of the Sicilian crime family. He'd made his way through six of Salvatore's best before he managed to corner him on a boat just off the shore of Palermo. As he kneeled waiting for the bullet to pass through his head, Giovanni had asked him one question.

"Is it true?"

"About?"

"What my mother said. Are you him?"

He paused then chuckled.

"The irony. To be shot by my own illegitimate child."

There was silence, then the cold metal pressed against the back of his skull was removed.

Salvatore had met his mother, Carina, in his early twenties. They had a whirlwind relationship only to have it cut short when her father learned about her involvement with him. He hadn't seen her since then. Almost twenty-five years had passed since that night. While the rumors had reached him, it took Carina another ten before she had the nerve to tell him through a letter that he had a son.

Over the following years he'd made every effort to ensure that she never went without. She lived in the best area of the city, all her expenses were paid, and in turn she was instructed that his son never be told who he was. She had obviously changed her mind.

There were very few things that he regretted in his life, but not being there for his son was one of them. The cost of being a part of the Sicilian Mafia was high. Most grew into it by family association. He didn't want that life for his child. And yet here he was years later looking into the eyes of one of the top hit men in Italy.

Fast and agile, in a period of nine years he'd notched up more kills than most of the other hit men combined. But it was the killing of seven men in a restaurant in the capital that had finally caught his attention. It was said that he'd entered, ordered some juice, and then without hesitating pulled two Para-Ordnance P18.9's and opened fire. So much blood was spilled that day, he soon became known as one of the most feared and well-paid hit men in the region.

The waiter came over and placed a white cup down.

Salvatore snapped back into the present.

"I'm sorry for your loss," Giovanni said. "Tell me what I can do to help."

He reached down into a brown leather bag, and pulled out a folder. He slid it across the table to him. Giovanni nursed his coffee, steam spiraling up from it as he opened the folder and looked at the face of Jack Winchester.

Salvatore could hear him flipping through pages.

"One man did all of this?"

"Does that surprise you?"

"No."

He continued reading, taking sips of his drink every few minutes. There was a refinement to everything he did. He was clean, exact and Salvatore knew that the job would be done. Over all the years he'd known him, there hadn't been one hit that had gone wrong. What made him deadly wasn't the body count. It was that he wasn't concerned with whether a kill was up close and personal or from one hundred yards. It was all about getting the job done. There was little ego involved.

"How much are you willing to pay?"

"Money is not an issue. You will be set up with an account. I want your full attention to be on this."

"Do you want him brought to you?"

"No. Make it clean. I don't want this to be traced back."

"Anything else?"

"Yes." His eyes flitted up. "Make it slow."

Chapter 3

Rain pelted the asphalt turning it into a slick black river. It was the beginning of what would become Hurricane Danielle. It was a little after eleven at night when a black SUV's gleaming headlights cut through the darkness before coming to a screeching halt a short distance from the emergency entrance to New Orleans East Hospital.

The rear door opened and a body was thrust into the gutter. She let out a pitiful whimper not just because her head smashed the side of the curb but because she had suffered far worse pain. Bleeding, and only wearing bra and panties, she tried to summon the strength to get up as the SUV sped away splashing dirty water all over her. She coughed and spluttered but could barely manage to lift her head.

Stunned and still in shock, her body lay in the flow of water that was trying to make its way down one of the many drains. The cold slapped her awake. Her face felt swollen, and the pain between her legs, well it was agonizing.

Digging deep, she forced herself up onto her knees and crawled up onto the curb. Rolling over on the concrete she lay there staring up at the black sky full of stars. How had it come to this? Did he know about this? Her immediate thoughts went to her child. Was she safe?

"Ma'am?" a voice said from behind her. She twisted over to see what looked like a security guard. His face widened in horror at the sight of her. She couldn't even begin to imagine what she looked like. All she felt was excruciating pain.

"I'll be right back."

She tried to mutter the words *don't leave* but it came out as garbled noise. Drifting in and out of consciousness she was sure she was going to die. Seconds, minutes, perhaps an hour passed before a crowd appeared at her side. With both eyes badly swollen she could barely make out who they were. Fear gripped her at the thought of her attackers returning.

"It's okay. Calm down. We're medics."

Over the course of the next few minutes all she felt was them placing her on a stretcher and then bumping around. Was she being taken to a hospital? Was this just a dream?

The sound of beeping echoed in her mind as the medics yelled different medical terminology. Nothing made sense. She was certain she would die. Darkness crept in at the sides of her eyes as they wheeled her into the hospital and bright fluorescent lights stung her eyes. A mask covered her mouth and she felt the rush of air fill her lungs. She was able to breathe better but the pain didn't let up.

"What have we got?"

"Security guard found her on his way into work."

"Ma'am, can you tell us who did this to you?"

She muttered a few words, none of them coherent or clear, though to her they made sense. The sound of nurses bustling. The aroma of hand sanitizer. A blue and white curtain running along rails. All of it mixed together like some surreal nightmare that she couldn't wake from.

"What is your name?"

She didn't reply so they repeated the question.

Eventually after the third, or perhaps the fourth time, she muttered, "Theresa."

"Did anyone get that?"

They asked again and she repeated it, this time a little louder.

"Okay, Theresa, do you have any allergies?"

Again they rambled off medical terminology, falling back on their training and making sure that she wouldn't have any reaction to the meds they would pump her body with. Morphine? Fluids? The world around her was beginning to get cloudy. Her mind circled back and forth between the horror of what had occurred, her daughter and then Jack.

* * *

The trill of birds and the sound of shopkeepers opening their stores was the first thing Jack heard that morning. He rolled over, his fingers gripped at the bedsheet. There was a moment in between sleep and being fully awake that felt good, a brief period of time he didn't remember his life, or the horrors of his past. It was peaceful, a clean slate, a mind absent of wrongdoing. He groaned as he glanced at the clock. It was a little after eight. His head throbbed from the aftermath of alcohol. Pushing back the covers he slid out of bed. The balls of his feet touched the cold, bare tiled floor. He breathed in deeply, letting life flood his lungs and mind. Light seeped through the shades over his windows. Since arriving in New Orleans he had contemplated taking on a job as a driver or in a kitchen, somewhere he could work for money under the table. While he wasn't desperate for money, his funds were slowly dwindling and he'd eventually have to find a way to put food on the table.

After taking a piss and splashing water over his face he slid back onto the bed and reached out for his laptop. Without the blinds open, the bright light from the computer stung his pupils. He accessed some of the local news as he did each day. It wasn't what was going on in the world that was of interest to him, as much as it was the cases that usually would be skimmed over by regular folk. It had become a habit, one that he was sure Eddie would have approved — finding those who needed help, the lost, the overlooked, the ones who fell through the cracks of the justice system.

The problem was that for all his searching, it was hard to distinguish those who really needed help from those who had brought trouble upon themselves. That's why a week ago he'd decided to place an ad in craigslist. It was simple and straight to the point.

Got a problem?

If the police or lawyers can't help perhaps I can.

Call me toll free. There is no obligation and everything will remain private.

The number that was left in the ad connected to voicemail that he used through a VOIP service. Jack

DEBT COLLECTOR: HARD TO KILL

checked in on it twice a day. Once in the morning and once at night. It couldn't be traced back to him and no details about who he was were ever given out in the ad or over the phone when he contacted people. That morning when he accessed his voice messages there was one message.

Hello?

Uh, I don't know how this works or if you can even help but I would like to talk. My name is Judith Frasier. Please call me back.

She left her phone number. It would be the first time he had replied to an ad. There had been others he'd received that he had just deleted. He wasn't sure why, perhaps nerves about the unknown. He dialed in the number using the VOIP service and waited.

"Hello?"

He hesitated for a moment. "You responded to my ad."

Chapter 4

A month had passed and Special Agent Isabel Baker was no closer to finding Jack Winchester. Daniel Cooper, the special agent she worked with in L.A., was still recovering and wouldn't be back for at least another month. He had phoned her from the hospital to see if Isabel would be interested in giving him a bed bath. The guy hadn't lost his sense of humor even with his near-death experience.

The first few days after getting out of the hospital she had interviewed John Dalton and Deon Smith, and spent a considerable amount of time spinning wheels in Chinatown. None of it had turned up anything. He had simply vanished like a ghost.

That was until she visited the Greyhound Bus Station on Seventh Street. For days she had worked her way through hours upon hours of footage of people coming and going. The problem with the surveillance was no cameras focused at the area where people paid. There were two cameras that showed people getting on and off buses, that was it.

Isabel had thought of quitting. Just contacting her superior, Simon Thorpe, and having him take her off the case. It had nearly killed her before and if Detective Frank Banfield was right, the chances of being able to outsmart Jack were low.

With a cup of coffee in hand she sat in her hotel room going through the security footage. She stared intently as more and more people got on and off buses. There was something about him that bothered her. Why had he not killed her? If he didn't leave behind anyone that had seen his face, why didn't he just finish off what Sheng Ping's men had started?

She was still lost in thought when she hit the pause button. Hope rose in her heart, then sank. It was a false alert. It really looked like him. The jacket, the height, the color of his hair but it wasn't. The image of his face was burned in her mind. The way he looked when they confronted him. She ran a hand over her tired face and pressed continue. It was going to be another long day.

While the grainy video played, showing the two bus bays, her phone rang. It was Cooper.

"Now I'm not going to wash you, massage you or anything else."

He chuckled on the other end of the line.

"Are you still going through that footage?"

She yawned. "Yep."

"You are wasting your time. That's like trying to find a needle in a haystack. He could have left days, even weeks after."

"What do you suppose I do? I have Thorpe breathing down my neck to find him."

"Contact Banfield."

She shook her head, pausing the video so she could focus on the call.

"Why would I do that? It's not like he was a barrel of insights."

"Perhaps he knew someone that Jack once knew. Let's

face it. The guy hasn't lived outside of New York other than when he was in Rockland Cove. Perhaps he has returned to New York."

"I don't think he would be that dumb."

"Ask Bundy, he returned to the scene of his crimes."

She stifled a laugh. "Cooper, we're not tracking a serial killer here."

"Are you sure about that?"

It was a valid point. He might not have hunted women for pleasure but he certainly had a long list of kills. It made her wonder if he found pleasure in the lives he took?

"When are you getting out?"

"Why, you miss me?"

"Like a dose of Ebola."

"Oh, that's cold," Cooper replied.

"No, I could use the extra help. You know, someone to run and do a few errands."

"By errands you mean, get you coffee and be your personal bitch."

She let out a laugh. "Hey, you said it. But now that you put it that way. Sure."

"Listen, if you get a lead, let me know. I am bursting for a reason to get out of this bed. The food sucks here and no one listens."

Isabel sat thinking for a few seconds after she got off the phone. Maybe she was going about this the wrong way. She swung her legs over the side of the bed and went over to her suitcase. She pulled out a case file to get the number of Detective Banfield.

She hesitated for a moment before phoning. Her last conversation with him didn't go over too well. She figured he would hang up on her the moment she spoke. The phone rang a few times before he answered.

"Detective Banfield."

"You really should get caller ID."

"Shit. Not you again."

"Look, I'm not going to take up much of your time."

"He got away from you, didn't he?" Banfield chuckled which only pissed her off.

"Your admiration of him is rather troubling, detective."

"It's not admiration, agent. Though I do find it amusing. So tell me, how did it happen?"

"We were ambushed from behind, otherwise your ghost would have been in cuffs."

He sighed. "So why are you calling me?"

"Do you think he might return to New York?"

"Not if he has any sense."

"You wouldn't harbor a fugitive, would you, detective?"

"This conversation is over."

"Hold on. Look, I just need a break here. Is there anyone he knows outside of New York?"

"Sorry, but I can't help you."

"Can't or won't?"

"Why are you still after him?"

She breathed in deeply. "To be quite honest, I'm asking myself that."

There was a pause as if both of them were

contemplating her answer.

Banfield sighed. "He had girlfriend, a long time ago. Word has it she moved to Louisiana."

"Her name?"

"Theresa Rizzo."

"Thank you, detective."

"Before you go. Question for you. Have your superiors told you why they want him?"

"Somewhat."

"Makes you wonder, doesn't it?"

"What?"

"If they are working in your best interest or their own."

She stifled a laugh. The thought had passed through her mind. It was part of the reason she had left the police department and joined the bureau. It was all politics and egos. She thought that things in the FBI would be different — they weren't.

Chapter 5

Billy Dixon had been out of prison only a week when he was scooped up by Tex's men. He kind of figured they would come knocking, he just thought he would have more time to get things back on track before they did.

Squished into the back seat with a handgun pointed at him, he stared at the two men keeping an eye on him while the other drove through the streets of Covington, Louisiana. After a few minutes one of them placed a black bag over his head and the rest of the journey he couldn't see a damn thing. But it didn't matter, he knew where he was going. He knew who he was going to see. The one person that no one got to see unless they had screwed up.

Charley Wilson, or Tex as most referred to him, was behind nearly all distribution of meth. While he never got involved in the actual distribution, he was the one that kept the business ticking over in these parts.

Below him were those that worked for him. For close

to six years Billy had only ever met them to pick up new supplies, drop off money or alert them to anyone flying solo. Flying solo was a term that was used for anyone making meth themselves.

It was common. Like, it wasn't hard to do. Every ingredient that was needed could be bought from the local drugstore. Things like brake fluid, rubbing alcohol, the lithium from batteries and the main ingredient pseudoephedrine were all easily accessible. Though with the law clamping down on how much pseudoephedrine could be purchased from drugstores, people had to get a little creative on how they obtained it. One person could now buy only nine grams per month legally. Most would work in crews of two or more to obtain more.

What had started out as a simple way to get more had turned into a full-time gig for Billy. He soon realized that he could pocket much more with his own team. It wasn't long before word got back to Tex, but by that time Billy had been pulled in on possession and sentenced to one year. That year had flown by and there wasn't a day inside that he hadn't thought about what the repercussions would be. He'd already received a visit while in jail from Tex's men who told him he owed a lot of money and they would be waiting for him when he got out.

Once he might have tried to run but he had her to think about now. He wasn't going to lose Theresa over his own stupidity. In some ways he thought he could talk his way out of it. That had always been his strong point. The gift of the gab, was what Theresa called it. He'd used it to his advantage many times inside, now he was about to find out if it worked on Tex.

The car rumbled making several turns and stops before it arrived. As Billy was dragged from the back of the car, he glanced down and could see he was being led along a dock. Fear crept over him at the thought of being thrown to alligators. He had seen Tex's men do it before to a guy who owed as little as ten thousand. He knew that his debt was far greater than that.

It was how Tex had managed to instill fear in those that worked for him. He didn't kill behind closed doors.

He would invite his main distributors to a location in the bayou and then have each of them kill someone. Everything was recorded. In the event they wanted to rat on him, the video of the killing would find its way to the police. He ruled in fear and intimidation, and it worked.

Billy wished he'd never met the man. But like anyone who was good at controlling others, Tex's introduction to himwas subtle. He was working for Tex long before he was told who his boss was. In the early days his uncle had been his source of meth ingredients and he worked for him distributing meth to locals. When his uncle was taken out of the picture a new supplier came into the game and he was the only one that could get his hands on large amounts of pseudoephedrine without the police breathing down his neck.

Whoever had access to large amounts of that was God around these parts.

Gradually the wood beneath Billy's feet turned to soil as he was led through brush and then into a building with concrete floors. He could hear voices but was unable to distinguish what they were saying. A few seconds passed before he was thrown to his knees and the bag was torn from his head. He blinked and squinted as the world around him came into view.

He was in a warehouse. Large blue canisters lined the sides of the walls. It had to be a storage facility or one of the many meth labs.

"Billy Dixon," a voice said.

Billy hadn't seen Tex in over three years. The last time he had, it was when Tex fed someone to alligators. As he stepped into view, Billy swallowed hard. Tex was a large man. Bald and looked as if he had eaten one too many burgers. While everyone knew he had more money than he could ever need, he didn't come across as someone who had wealth. There was a reason for that. Rumor had it that he gained the trust of people by looking like he was making the same amount of cash they were. He wore a jean shirt, cowboy boots and had dark hair that was swept back with some kind of hair product that looked like grease. The aroma of some cheap aftershave filled the air.

"Hey Tex."

"How was it inside?"

"You know. It's prison."

He nodded without a grin on his face.

"How long were you working for me before you went in?"

Billy shook his head trying to remember. Fear had clouded out any clear thought.

"Six years?"

"Something like that."

"Didn't I pay you well?"

"Yeah. Yeah you did."

"And, didn't I make sure your family was looked after?"

Billy didn't reply. His hesitation caused one of Tex's men to slap the side of his face from behind to get a response out of him. He felt his skin sting.

"That's right. You did."

"So tell me. Whatever went through your mind to think that you could steal from me?"

"I wasn't stealing. I was giving you exactly what you asked for."

"Seventy-five percent."

"Exactly."

"But that's not what I heard you were pulling in. Word has it you had your own little enterprise."

Billy's eyes darted around the room as a few more men came into view. One of them had a knuckle duster on and he was rubbing it against his open hand and licking his lips with anticipation. A cold shot of fear flooded his being as he saw another one holding the end of a chain that was dangling from a free hand.

"Please, Tex, I can make this right."

"Twenty thousand dollars is what I figure you owe me. Give or take a few dollars here or there."

"I can get it for you."

He stepped forward and crouched down in front of Billy with his arms resting against his knees. "What? You have a bank account or stash of money that I don't know about?"

"No."

"Then how do you suppose you are going to repay me?"

"I have connections."

He chuckled and patted the side of Billy's face gently, looking at his men before he stood up. "He has connections. Billy Dixon has connections. Well, that concludes our conversation then. If you have connections I have nothing to worry about, right?"

"Right."

"But that's the thing, Billy. Everyone who owes me money, says the same thing. I'll get it to you next month, next week, tomorrow. And the money never arrives." He paused for effect. "Now, I'm a fair man. At least, I like to think so. Now before you started your little enterprise, I have to admit, you were making me a fair bit of coin."

Billy started to feel a glimmer of hope.

"I don't want to lose the additional money, especially since I have lost a lot since you were incarcerated. So here's what I'm going to do. You have forty-eight hours to come up with forty thousand dollars."

"But you said I owe you twenty?"

"You do. But you've been inside for a year and that has cost me even more, and then of course there is interest. I figure forty thousand is a nice round figure that should cover what you owe me."

"I can't come up with that kind of money in two days!"

Tex stopped pacing around him and came up real close, to the point that Billy could feel his warm breath against his face.

"Are you sure about that?"

He nodded.

"Is that your final answer?"

Billy frowned. Did he think this was a game? He'd heard the rumors about Tex. One minute he could act calm and nice, the next he would cut your throat.

"I just mean I need a bit more time. Like a week or two."

"I've been waiting over a year and you want me to wait

a week or two?"

"If I had the money I would give it to you now."

Tex studied his face.

"You had the money, you didn't give it to me. Why should I believe anything that comes out of your mouth?"

Billy searched for words, anything to convince him that he was good for it. He stuttered a little and mumbled but his mind went blank. Tex rose to his feet and with just a simple nod to his men they charged him and began beating on him. The first punch with the knuckle duster knocked one of his teeth out. The chain to his body tore his shirt and cut into his flesh. The assault lasted for a few minutes before Tex called off his dogs.

Billy spat blood on the floor and pleaded with him. "Okay, okay, I can get the money."

Tex let out a deep belly laugh. "Of course you can. Stand him up."

His men brought Billy to his feet. The back of his legs and lower back burned with pain. Blood trickled down the side of his eye and lip. Tex brushed the dust off him as if he was dealing with a young child who had returned home muddy. He slapped the sides of his arms.

"There's a price we all have to pay, Billy. Forty-eight hours."

He nodded, relieved that Tex was at least giving him a chance. Even so, he knew it was useless. He couldn't come up with that kind of money. Fresh out of prison, he no longer had his team to sell.

Tex gave a nod to his men and they covered his head with the bag and were about to lead him away when Tex spoke again.

"And Billy. If you are thinking of running. Don't. My grace won't be extended twice."

With that he was led away and they returned him to where they had taken him. The door to the car opened and he was shoved out onto the hard concrete.

The squeal of tires and the smell of burning rubber assaulted his senses.

* * *

Tex had waited until Billy was out of earshot before he

called over his son Kalen.

"See to it that he gets a clear message."

"You want him dead?"

"No."

"His family?"

He nodded.

"Why not just kill him?"

"Kalen," Tex wrapped his hand around his son's head. "I know you might not understand this now but what I'm trying to build here will eventually be handed over to you. The hardest part about what we do is decide who lives and dies. I could have killed him but he's more profitable to me alive."

"But you've killed people for less."

"They didn't bring in the amount of money that Billy has. We don't want to shoot ourselves in the foot. Everyone makes mistakes, you job is to decide if it's ultimately going to affect your end game."

"Which is?"

"To get out."

Kalen frowned. "You've lost me."

Tex breathed in deeply, placed his arm around his son and began walking around the building. "Look around you. This is all just a means to an end. Contrary to what some might think, I don't enjoy doing this. It pays well. It gives me the lifestyle I want. But it comes with its own risk. Ten years ago this business was very different. With the law cracking down on the sale of pseudoephedrine, it's only going to be a matter of time before all of the states require a prescription."

"So? You'll find another way to get it."

"Of course. But if it means going to prison, no. I'm in this to get what I want out of it and then we move on."

"I don't understand you, Father. You've worked your whole life to build this business, to gain the respect of those around you and you want to just throw it away?"

Tex let out a laugh and smiled. "You'll understand one day."

It was hard to explain to his son that which only experience and time could teach him. He was first and foremost a businessman, not a drug lord, no matter how people looked at him. And like any good businessman he weighed the pros and cons. He considered carefully the risk factor. Creating methamphetamine had made him a wealthy man, but it had become addictive. The thrill of earning hundreds of thousands of dollars wasn't easy to walk away from. At one time when he was younger, he would have never imagined getting out of the business. But business was different back then. Now it was a cutthroat operation. Anyone with access to a drugstore and household supplies could go into business for themselves. If anything, what Billy had taught him was that it was getting harder to control those around him. Everyone wanted a piece of the pie. It wouldn't be long before the Mexican cartel would run the show, and well, from there it would all be downhill.

Chapter 6

Before meeting with Judith Frasier, Jack decided to head over to the hotel Theresa was working at. While he didn't expect their relationship to pick up where they had left off, he wanted to make sure she was financially doing okay. He couldn't help feel responsible for some of the trouble and danger he'd placed her in years ago.

While he had dated a lot of women, few had been as supportive as Theresa had. Perhaps that was because they came from similar backgrounds. They had originally met through Gafino. She was dancing in one of his bars and barely scraping by with the tips she was getting from lap dances. Most of Gafino's guys saw the dancers as nothing more than sluts. But they were hard-working; many had kids and were just doing whatever they could to get by. Theresa was one of them. A runaway. She had spent the first part of her teenage years on the street as a working girl until Gafino found her and put her to work in his club. It was tough to say whether that was a good thing or not. Certainly there was less chance of her getting beaten by a trick but she still had to service clients. If she wasn't dancing or performing lap dances she was tending to the needs of his VIP clients.

Call it chance, or whatever, when Jack met her on the Fourth of July, he knew there was more to her than a great body. She was damaged inside, much like him. She carried her scars like souvenirs, each one a thorny memento on the stem of her rose-colored life. Each one a reminder of her strength. At least that's what she said. Jack found it hard to find strength in what he had been through. The years of abuse at the hands of his father, the manipulation by a mob boss weren't so much scars as they were deep wounds that had never healed.

It wasn't long before he was spending more time with her than focusing on work. Gafino soon noticed and made clear in no uncertain terms that they would never be an item. She was just merchandise, another cog in the wheel of his empire that was fueled by greed.

As Jack threaded his way down the busy street heading for the hotel, he thought back to the first day out of jail and Gafino's off-the-cuff remark about the woman he was banging looking a lot like Theresa. Knowing that Jack liked her, Gafino had made a point to have Theresa service him multiple times. He had taken Jack to the club, and asked for her right in front of him. At first Jack thought Gafino was arranging for him to have some alone time with her, that idea was squashed when he watched Gafino walk into the back room with her.

That night Jack got a lap dance from some girl whose name he couldn't remember. Frustration overtook him and he walked in on them in the middle of Theresa taking care of business. It had been the only time that Jack had come close to killing his own boss.

If it weren't for the fact that there was no one else who could have filled his shoes, he was pretty sure Gafino would have disposed of him. Instead, he respected the guts it took at a young age to challenge him. Gafino never touched Theresa again. It wasn't that he couldn't have, he chose not to. That's when the relationship developed. Jack got her out of the club and she stayed at his place until four years before he went into jail.

She would say the relationship was doomed from the start but he never saw it that way. She was the first one to plant a seed that his life could be different, that he didn't have to work for the mob. While Dana watered that idea later, Theresa had been there from the beginning. She knew the risk involved of walking away from the mob. It was the reason why when he refused to leave, she gave him an ultimatum. Leave with her, or it was over.

She left, and Jack continued working for Gafino for another four years.

Upon his arrival at the French-style hotel, Mazarin on Bienville Street, the five-story building loomed over him. Dark clapboard shutters were on either side of the windows. He'd considered staying there but after his first run-in with Theresa, he figured it might have been awkward. All the rooms on the second floor had iron balconies. Everything about the place was luxurious. The sound of jazz could be heard just half a block away on Royal Street. Inside, a crystal chandelier illuminated the lobby. A well-dressed clerk eyed him while speaking to one of the guests. Jack glanced down at his clothes. He wasn't exactly dressed for a place like this. His appearance looked rugged with a leather jacket, jeans and boots. His face had five days of growth and no doubt the dark circles around his eyes made him look a little shifty.

"Can I help you, sir?"

"Yes. I was hoping to speak to Theresa."

"Oh, I'm afraid she's not in today."

"Do you know when she'll be back?"

The man looked uncomfortable. He stepped out back and looked around then reappeared.

"Look, I'm a friend of hers."

He hesitated before he replied. "I really shouldn't be telling you this. Someone phoned last night to say that she had been admitted into the hospital."

"Hospital? Why?"

"I'm not sure but it didn't sound good."

"Which one?"

"East."

Before the man could say any more, Jack was already out the door. His pulse was racing and his heart was pounding in his chest. The thought that his presence in New Orleans might have placed her in danger made him fraught with worry. He thumbed a taxi and hopped in.

"Where are we going?"

He gave the address, told him to hurry and the cabdriver gunned the engine. Inside he peered around at the many voodoo objects dangling from pins. The driver was black with long dreadlocks. He was the spitting image of Bob Marley.

"Name's Jamaar."

Jack didn't reply.

"So how do you like the Crescent City?"

Jack barely registered what he had said.

"What?"

"Sorry, people have trouble with my accent. I'm not from around here."

I would have never guessed, Jack thought before glancing out the window as the buildings blurred in his peripheral vision.

"I came up here for a better life. It's a mess down in Jamaica. Not what my father said it used to be. Here I get to drive people around, I make great tips and well, it's never a dull moment, right?"

"Right," Jack replied lost in thought. "You think you can go a little faster?"

"Yah mon."

Chapter 7

Giovanni arrived at John F. Kennedy a little after ten in the morning. He felt refreshed after flying first class on a non-stop from Italy. He brought no weapons with him. Salvatore had already made the call to his associates to provide him with everything he would need.

This would be the first time he had stepped on U.S. soil. Since receiving the details of who he was going to kill, he hadn't given much thought to the job. He rarely gave much thought to contracts. Others in his profession would become obsessed with a job. He never saw the point. Until they were standing across from you, they were not a threat. And most often he didn't wait until they could see him before he killed. Though this time it had to be different. It would have been a lie to say that he wasn't concerned. Getting up close and personal was not his first choice. Killing from a distance was his preference. There was no room for ego. Ego was how so many in his line of work had been killed.

He thought about a good friend of his who had racked up quite a body count. He'd been paid handsomely for his ability to extinguish lives. The trouble was he'd begun to grow tired of his own method of killing victims from a distance. He wanted to change things up. Get up close and see the look of horror in their eyes when they knew they were about to die.

For a while it had worked. He left a trail of blood and fear behind him that was felt among many of the crime families, until he bit off more than he could chew.

His final target before he died was to kill Giovanni.

Giovanni had learned about the hit twenty-four hours before it was meant to go down. He wasn't bothered by the fact that it was his friend. It was to be expected. Giovanni had stepped on one too many toes. He had become a threat to many.

Had he taken the shot from a distance, perhaps his friend would have been the one arriving in the United States. Instead he was now buried in an unmarked grave in Palermo.

Ego had killed more friends than he cared to mention.

That's what worried him about this job.

Unless required, he remained hidden, a ghost, someone who killed from a distance.

Regardless, in his mind this would be a simple in and out job. He'd listened to what Salvatore had said about this man, he'd read over the file. He figured he was no more dangerous than those he had gone up against before, and he had faced some of Italy's most deadly hit men.

As he came out of the airport doors with no more than a carry-on case, he was greeted by a short Italian man holding up a sign with his name on it. Before guiding him into the parking lot, the man asked if he wanted to get a drink. He declined. He wasn't here for socializing. There was a lot to be done if he was to find Jack Winchester. Finding them was the hardest part, after that it was no different than removing the cork on a bottle of pinot red wine.

"An associate of mine will visit you with the goods.

Details of the last-known associate can be found in a folder on the passenger seat."

Giovanni held out his hand for the keys. The pudgy man hesitated before he gave them.

"Don't you have any questions?"

"No."

With that he took the keys to a silver Aston Martin Vanquish. He eyed the man as he slipped behind the wheel. Inside it smelled of fresh, untouched leather. He briefly glanced at the folder before turning over the ignition. It roared to life. As the throaty, well-tuned engine idled, he flipped the folder open. At the top was a photo of Detective Banfield along with his home address. He adjusted the mirrors, backed out and gunned it.

* * *

Jack hurried down the hospital corridor towards the main front desk. All manner of thoughts rushed through his mind. Had she been shot? Been in a car crash? Did the FBI get to her? It was hard not to think that he was somehow responsible. Everyone he had crossed paths with or cared for, in some way or form had ended up hurt.

"She's in room 521."

"Thank you."

Shuffling along he noticed a woman selling flowers from a small trolley. He came up alongside her and fished in his pocket for a twenty-dollar bill. She handed him a small, hand-tied bouquet of pastel shades of pink, white, lilac and cream. He caught an aroma of their fragrance. As he came up to the door he peered inside, took a deep breath and entered.

Theresa didn't move, she was hooked up to all manner of tubes and her face was a dark shade of purple. She looked like she'd been hit with a car. An EKG monitor off to the right-hand side beeped away. Jack placed the flowers in a small empty vase that was on a counter, then filled it with water from the bathroom. The fact that there were no other flowers was strange. When he returned, her eyelids were open.

"Jack?"

"Hey," he said softly, standing there for a second

before moving to her side and placing the flowers down on her bedside table.

"Those for me?"

He tilted his head to one side. Her lip curled at the corner ever so slightly until she winced.

"How did this happen?" he asked as he pulled up a chair beside her bed and took a seat.

"Can I get some water?"

"Yeah. Yeah." He got up and returned with a glass half filled. He held it up to her cracked lips and she sipped at it. He couldn't believe the state she was in. Only a day earlier he'd seen her and her skin was perfect. Completely blemish-free and without flaw. Now it was discolored and patched up. Her lower lip was split, and both eyes looked as if she had been pummeled repeatedly. He could still see deep red finger marks on her throat.

"Who did this?"

She tried to sit up but groaned in agony. Jack looked at the bed and pressed one of the buttons to elevate the back. As she came up slowly he studied her.

"I uh, was on my way back to my car last night when a vehicle pulled up beside me. Two guys jumped out and threw me in the back. They put a bag over my head and we drove around for what seemed like maybe thirty minutes. I don't think they were going anywhere, I think they were trying to disorient me." She breathed in slowly. "Anyway, when the car stopped I was dragged into some building. I don't even know where it was. All I remember is it didn't smell good. Like it was full of chemicals or something like that. They removed the bag from my head and there were five people in the room. The four large guys I'm guessing were the muscle for the guy who spoke." She closed her eyes as if trying to recall. "He said it was my lucky night. That was it. It was my lucky night." She paused. "They raped me, then…" She barely managed to get the words out but Jack had a feeling he knew what she was going to say. "After which they just kept beating me, cutting me. They said if I told the police, they would do the same to my daughter."

"Daughter?"

Her eyes shifted over to Jack and she nodded.

"You never mentioned you had a child."

She never replied.

"Where's your boyfriend?"

"I didn't phone him."

"What?"

"I didn't want him to know about this."

Jack got up from his seat and paced back and forth.

"Theresa, you need to let him know."

"I can't tell him."

There was silence for a moment. "Where's your daughter?"

"She's with Billy."

"How do you know?"

"I asked a friend to check in."

"Don't you think he's going to get a little suspicious when you return with bruises all over you?"

She reached for the glass. Jack brought it over to her.

"What about the police? Have you contacted them?"

"They came by but I told them I couldn't remember.

They won't do anything about it anyway. In fact, by the questions they asked, I got a sense they thought I had brought it on myself."

"But you hold down a respectable job."

"I don't have a respectable past, now do I, Jack? Both you and I know it wouldn't take them long to bring that up and well…" Her eyes dropped before meeting his gaze. "I was wondering…"

Jack lifted a hand. "No. I can't get involved."

"Why? This is what you do. It's who you are."

"Not anymore. You need to go to the police on this. And anyway, you said yourself, you don't know where they took you or who they were."

"If I tell the police they will hurt her."

"How can you be sure this wasn't just a random incident? For all we know they do this all the time. Maybe they mistook you for a lost tourist?"

She stared at him.

"They knew my daughter's name. They knew her name was Ruby."

Jack breathed out a heavy sigh and leaned back in his chair.

"Did you have anything in your purse with her name?"

"No. Just a photo."

He stared blankly back at her. "Look, I'd like to help but—"

"She's your daughter, Jack," she cut him off. His eyes widened as he allowed the words to sink in. At first he didn't know what to say. She continued, "I should have phoned. But I…"

"If you are trying to get my help by lying…"

"I'm not lying. Look at the photo. It's in my bag."

Jack went over to a black leather bag that had a bloodstain on the side. He brought it over to her and she ferreted inside until she retrieved the photo. He looked at the girl who was the spitting image of her mother. She had dark hair and dark eyes. He tried to see the resemblance to himself but he couldn't see it. She was a good-looking kid.

"When did you have her?"

"Eight years ago."

"Four years before I went inside?"

She nodded. "I wanted us to get away from the life we were living."

"And you didn't think to tell me you were pregnant?"

"Would you have let me go if I had?"

He shook his head.

"I left for Ruby's sake, and mine. That wasn't a life to let her grow up in."

"And this is?"

Jack breathed in deeply as the weight of her confession bore down on him. He got up and walked to the door.

"Where are you going?"

"I need to get some air."

Chapter 8

The crime in New York never let up. Frank stood at a murder scene in an apartment. He gazed around at the mess. Even pigs lived better than this, he thought. It was like no one cared about hygiene anymore. He smeared Vicks VapoRub underneath his nostrils to prevent him tossing up his breakfast. It was late morning when the call came in. A typical domestic dispute had spiraled out of control between two neighbors over the noise of music. One of the neighbors had retrieved his Glock and unloaded four rounds into the couple living across from him, then turned the gun on himself and blew his brains out.

No one could get used to the sight of brain matter spread across the wall or the stench of bodies festering in the heat of day. As the crime team made their way around recording, photographing and dusting for prints, Frank found himself thinking about the conversation he'd had with Agent Baker. The woman didn't let up. But there was something different about her tone this time around. Something had changed. He could only hope that she came to her senses before it was too late. He wasn't worried that Jack would kill her. He didn't hurt women, at least that was the rumor.

"Have you interviewed the witnesses?" Frank asked a fellow officer.

"There was only one other person who was brave enough to stick their head outside the door. Even then, she said that he fired at her when she did. Thankfully she slammed the door in time otherwise we might have had a fourth victim."

"Any motive established?"

"According to the landlord, our guy was fired from his job yesterday."

Frank shook his head. It never ceased to amaze him even after all the years on the force, the lengths that people would go to when stressed. City life had a way of bringing out the worst in people. You could almost feel the stress and tension in the air as you journeyed through the mass of New Yorkers. It didn't take much for people to break down in the Big Apple. A sudden loss of work, someone cutting them off or even a look could be taken the wrong way. He knew it all too well. He was already taking meds for a lack of sleep. However, despite the stress he'd been under of late, he was just glad to have work. It kept his mind occupied.

"Listen, you think you can wrap this up? I have one more call to attend to and then I'm knocking off for the day."

"Lucky," Dave said. "It never ends for us."

"Yeah, you might want to rethink being a detective, it doesn't get much better."

He turned away and exited the building that smelled of urine, blood and death. Outside in the street he made his way over to his car and slid in. For a few seconds he didn't turn over the ignition, he just sat there and allowed his mind to find peace.

Though his peace was short-lived when he felt the cold

metal pressed against his temple. His eyes flitted up to the rearview mirror to see a stranger in the back of his car. For someone who was holding up a detective outside the scene of a crime with cops walking around, he was very calm and collected.

"Drive."

"Where?"

"Just start the car and go."

Frank moved ever so slowly while the man pulled out Frank's piece from inside his jacket. The car chugged to life and he guided it out as the man ducked down to avoid detection. When they had got a few blocks from the apartment the man gave him instructions to return to his home. Frank fell back on his negotiation techniques that he'd learned over the years in the hope that he could deter the man from pulling the trigger. He could tell the guy wasn't a junkie. He'd seen enough of them in his time. They had this wild look in their eyes, dark circles and usually were shaking because they needed money to get high. This guy was nothing like that. He acted as though this was just a walk in the park. That's what concerned Frank. He hadn't seen him around the city, and his face had never appeared in any photos that he could recall. Was he Mafia?

When they arrived outside his home, the man took the keys to the car and got out, then instructed him to step out. He kept the gun firmly fixed against the low part of his back. One shot and his spine would be ripped in two. If he was lucky he'd be sucking food through a straw and forever remain crippled. The alternative was death, neither of them were appealing.

"If you want money, I can give you that."

"Just get inside."

Frank's heart was racing as he tried to make sense of what was going on. He fumbled with the keys and dropped them.

"Pick 'em up."

Frank swallowed hard and reached down to grab them. For a brief second he considered slamming his fist into the guy's family jewels but with the gun aimed right at him, it would have been a risky move. He inserted the key and turned over the lock. When the door opened, the man shoved him forward into the living room.

"Take a seat."

Frank slumped down in an armchair and the man sat across from him. He didn't say anything for at least two minutes. He just sat observing Frank as if weighing up the risk. Laying the gun on the arm of the chair, but with his finger still against the trigger, he reached into his pocket and pulled out a packet of cigarettes.

"Cigarette?"

Was this guy mental? Clearly. "No."

"You don't mind?"

A kidnapper with manners?

"Go ahead."

He placed the cigarette between his lips and lit the end. It glowed a deep orange and then he blew out a puff of grey smoke and studied him.

"Jack Winchester. Where is he?"

Frank chuckled a little.

"Something amusing?"

"You're the second person today who has asked about him."

"Who else was asking?"

"FBI."

"And what did you tell them?"

Frank stared at him. The hesitation was a mistake.

The crack of the gun going off jolted him. It was followed by excruciating pain in his right foot. Either he thought Frank wasn't going to tell him or he wanted to prove a point that he wasn't messing around.

"What the hell?"

"What did you tell them?"

Through gritted teeth he replied, "I told her that he used to date a woman here in the city, by the name of Theresa Rizzo. She moved to Louisiana eight years ago."

Frank yanked off his shoe and wrapped his hands around his bloodied foot. He was groaning in agony as he looked for something to wrap around it.

"That won't be necessary," the stranger said as Frank

tried to get up. He motioned for him to take his seat again. In excruciating pain but not wanting to die, he did as he was told.

The man continued smoking his cigarette.

"No family?"

Frank shook his head.

"Do you know where Jack is?"

"I swear I don't. He was here about seven months ago, he went to L.A. and then well, who knows where he has gone."

"But you think he might have gone to Louisiana?"

"How the hell should I know?" he bellowed.

That was the wrong thing to say. He fired another shot into his left foot. The pain intensified and he knew this wouldn't end well.

"I've told you everything you want to know."

"How do you know what I want to know?"

"Well, you asked me about Jack."

"How do you know what I want to know?"

What kind of mind game was he playing with him?

"Who do you work for?" Frank asked. If he was going to die he at least wanted to know who sent him. Not that it mattered. The stranger didn't reply. He got up from his seat and stubbed out his cigarette. Then he removed from his pocket a small Ziploc bag and placed the cigarette stub into it. He pocketed it and proceeded to pick up the shells expelled from his Glock. They went into a separate bag and in his left pocket.

"Who do you work for?" Frank asked again.

The man didn't smile or make light of anything he was doing. He had no need to tell Frank anything, neither did he have any reason to keep him alive.

"You know if you are going after him you are making a big mistake."

Something in what Frank said caught his attention. The man came over to Frank as if he was about to do something. He then took his seat across from him.

"Tell me about Jack Winchester."

By now the pain level had become almost unbearable. The carpet was soaked in blood.

"What do you want to know?"

"Everything."

Frank stared back at him knowing that this was going to be his last day on earth. It had all come down to this. Years of doing what was right meant very little now. Could he have avoided this by locking Jack up? Maybe, maybe not. The Mafia cared very little about the level of involvement in an incident, only about who was considered a potential problem. Judges, police or another member of the crime syndicate, it didn't matter to those at the top. If you were a liability, nothing could protect you. Not even a witness protection program. Frank knew this when he became a cop. It was the reason why many officers chose to look the other way. It was the reason most officers didn't pursue advancement. It only meant dealing with more shit.

"So?"

Frank snorted a little at the irony of it all. He had always imagined that he would retire and spend the remainder of his days golfing or sipping an exotic drink down in the Florida Keys. He shook his head slowly, looking at the stranger. No, and the irony was, he wouldn't even know his killer.

"You're not going to tell me, are you?"

Frank smiled for a minute; a final act of defiance.

"No."

The last image he had was of his gun being raised, then everything went black.

Chapter 9

The image of him on the video was blurry at best. The information Frank had provided enabled her to filter down on a timeline that Greyhound buses left L.A. for Louisiana. From there she had watched lines of people stream in and out of buses. If it wasn't for a second camera she might have not spotted him. As the bus for New Orleans pulled out, it paused a few feet away, partially out of view. From the rear of the bus she saw a figure run up along the side. After she got the guys at the bureau to enhance it, they were able to get a shot of his face. She now knew where he was heading to in Louisiana and she had a name. It was the break she needed. Her boss would be pleased. Simon had been breathing down her neck for the past week. The guy had no idea. All he understood were results.

"Surely the bureau has another agent that can go with you?" Cooper asked.

"You would think so. No."

"Has Simon got in contact with the U.S. Marshals?"

"And set up a fugitive task force? No."

"You are joking. This doesn't make any sense."

"Of course it does. They are looking to cover their ass. We get the U.S. Marshals involved and the media gets wind of it, what happens then if they don't catch him? The bureau is going to look like complete fools. Never mind the fact that they are going to have to explain themselves to the powers that be."

It might have been hard for people to imagine that the FBI would risk the chance of losing Winchester just to save face but it wouldn't have been the first time the left hand didn't know what the right hand had done.

"I'm coming with you."

"Don't be stupid. Your doctor said you have at least another two months to heal."

"To heal, yes, but not to discharge me."

"No, I've been given strict instructions on this."

"What? He's keeping me out of the loop? I didn't just

take three bullets for nothing. I want this asshole as much as you do."

"Remember, it wasn't him who fired at you."

"It doesn't mean he's any less to blame. If we weren't occupied with him, we would have seen those men come in."

"Would have, should have."

"Are you serious?"

"If you are going to complain to Simon, save it for someone who gives a shit. I've already been down that path and it got me nowhere. They will just take us off the case and shuffle us into some godforsaken part of the country to work behind a desk."

Cooper sighed. "So what is new?"

She brought him up to speed on what Frank had told her.

"And the girl? Any luck with that?"

"I'm still waiting on an address and place of employment."

"What hotel are you going to be staying at?"

She told him and he made a comment about how he would book in there.

"Are you in a sling?"

"No, just bandaged up. The wounds have been healing nicely. I've got a stack of pain meds."

"To be honest, Cooper, I think you might just slow me down."

He went quiet.

"What can I do then?"

"Well, I already have a flight booked for late this evening. If you could follow up with the head office and let me know when they've got that address, that would help."

"I still can't believe they are not getting the U.S. Marshals involved."

"There's a lot I don't believe about the bureau but one thing is for sure, I'm not going to question their instructions. I want this guy and if I have to bring him in alone, so be it."

After hanging up, Isabel began packing her belongings.

She tossed back a few pain meds that she'd been given for her own gunshot wound. Contrary to what most might have thought, recovery from a gunshot wound was different for everyone. There were a lot of factors involved. How healthy a person was, their age and the path the bullet took all factored into how quickly a person might get discharged. Two weeks was common, longer if bones were shattered. She was fortunate, Cooper not so. A bullet had torn through a bone and there was a strong chance he was going to have to use a cane for life. Of course he wouldn't admit it. Typical guy. But the probability of him returning to fieldwork was small. He would have to pass a secondary medical examination before they could determine if he was ready. Isabel had already jumped through the hoops and been given the clear. She'd entertained the thought of returning to being a cop in San Francisco numerous times. She never imagined that was something she would ever want to do again but after all the political bullshit she had experienced, she wasn't sure now.

She phoned down to the front desk to let them know that she would be checking out and could they finalize all charges and send the invoice on to the office. When she hung up she cast her eyes around the room. A deep sense of loneliness took a hold of her. In all her efforts to advance her career, she hadn't truly considered the cost. There had been no time to develop any relationship. It wasn't like she hadn't had numerous opportunities but they always ended up being one-night stands. It wasn't the guy who left in the morning, it was her. In the heat of the moment under the intoxication of passion and alcohol, she would imagine what it would be like to have a normal life. It wasn't like anyone was stopping her. There were tons of cops and FBI agents that came home to a family but she had always had her eye on the ball. The only way to climb the ladder, her father would say, was through pure grunt work. You have to do what others aren't willing to do, to get where others won't get. It had become almost a mantra to her. But in the past few years that mantra had begun to wear thin. She wasn't getting any younger. If she wanted to have kids, now was the time.

As she continued packing, her phone started buzzing on the side table and shifting around. She walked over still folding her clothes. She glanced down at the caller ID and saw it was Simon.

"Sir?"

"When did you last speak to Frank Banfield?"

She frowned for a minute wondering how he had known about her call. She hadn't told him.

"Yesterday."

"He's been found dead in his apartment. Execution style."

Her mouth widened a little as she soaked in the news. Her heartbeat increased a little.

"You think Jack did it?"

"Cops don't know right now. There were no witnesses. No one heard anything."

"CTV?"

"Not in that area."

Isabel took a seat on the edge of the bed and pinched the bridge of her nose feeling a tension headache coming on.

"You don't want me to go to New York, do you?"

"No, we'll have the branch there handle it. You need to find this man and find him quickly."

"But what if he's there?"

"Then I guess someone else will do your job for you."

She clenched her jaw. Simon was about to hang up when she asked another question.

"Cooper is being discharged, he wants to get back on the case."

There was a pause.

"You don't think he's up to it?"

"That's not for me to decide. He has to be cleared medically but..."

"You don't think he's up to it," he repeated himself.

She exhaled hard. "It's my not my place to say. Look, have you got anyone else you can send with me? Who knows what I'm going into here. Also, why aren't the

U.S. Marshals getting involved here?"

"They are."

"Oh," she said, her eyebrows rising.

"So there's a task force that you can put me in contact with?"

"Just leave that to me. Right now get yourself to Louisiana."

Chapter 10

It took a lot of convincing to get Theresa to call her husband. When Billy Dixon showed up, Jack wasn't sure what he was expecting to see. By the way Theresa talked about him, Jack assumed he would be dressed in business attire. What he imagined was far from it. Billy wore a red plaid sleeveless shirt, his arms were covered in tattoos and his jeans were torn up. He was also sporting a black eye and a cut lip. Jack was sitting in a chair when he came in. He wasn't in the direct line of sight when Billy came in and went over to Theresa.

"Baby, what the hell?" He wrapped his hands around her face and kissed her forehead. As he stepped back he saw Jack out the corner of his eye.

"Who are you?"

"Billy, this is an old friend of mine, Jack Winchester."

"You never told me about him. Why are you here?"

Jack never said anything, he just let them talk between

themselves while he stepped out. There was no yelling or tears to be heard, just the quiet murmur of voices. When Billy stepped out into the hallway he looked pitiful.

"She says you've helped her in the past. Is that true?"

He nodded.

"I appreciate that." He stepped in a little closer. "But what are you doing here?"

"Better question. Where's Ruby?"

"She's with a friend of ours."

Jack nodded. "Do you know who might have wanted to do this?"

"I have a good idea."

"Give me a name."

He looked Jack up and down. "What are you? A cop?"

Jack stifled a laugh. "What do you do for a living, Billy?"

A look spread across his face. "I just got out. Couple of weeks ago."

"How long were you inside?"

"A year."

"For what?"

"Misdemeanor crime. What's it to you?"

A doctor passed by and the gap between them widened. Jack could feel the tension. He knew Billy wasn't seeing him as the old friend who had just come into the picture. No doubt he was wondering how long Jack had been in the picture. How long had Jack been seeing his woman? Jack pursed his lips and bit down on the side of his inner cheek, keeping his eyes on Billy as the corridor filled up with nurses and patients. He motioned with a nod for them to step into another room. They entered a small waiting area where a kid sat on the floor playing with toys while a young mother tapped away on her smartphone oblivious to them.

"Who did you piss off?"

"What do you mean?"

"Before you got put away, who were you working for? I'm guessing the misdemeanor was drug related?" He paused waiting for Billy to jump in. He didn't, which only annoyed Jack even more. Instead Billy took a seat and got this worried look all over his face.

"Look, I used to deal in methamphetamine for some guy but I don't do it anymore. I'm trying to go straight, you know." He paused. "For Theresa and Ruby."

Jack could relate to that. "So?"

"When I got out, they approached me for the money I owed them."

"How much?"

He hesitated before he replied. "Forty grand. I told them I was good for it but they…" He pointed to his face.

"Looks like you got off lightly."

"They did this, didn't they?"

His head dropped.

"Did you know?"

"No. Do you think I would have allowed them to touch her? I just thought they were empty threats. You know, to scare me."

"How long have they given you?"

"Forty-eight hours."

"Or what?"

He stared back at Jack. Jack didn't need him to answer, he already knew. This was the kind of work he had to do back in the city. Though he never roughed up a woman or child, he knew that some of Gafino's men had. Some would say it wasn't personal, just business. That was bullshit. It was always personal. Any loss of money was a jab to the ego. People had to be taught a lesson. Theresa was the lesson. They didn't bother roughing Billy up too much, they knew they could get their point across more effectively by hurting those he cared for. It was an old-school approach. Some people would take all manner of beatings and threats on their life but threaten their family and you soon had their attention.

"So what are you going to do?" Jack asked. The woman across from them must have overheard as she scooped up her child and briskly walked out of the room looking concerned. The door closed slowly behind her and it was just the two of them. Billy scratched his forehead leaving a red mark just above his eye.

"I don't know. I can't come up with that kind of cash."

Jack didn't bother to ask if he had thought of running away. That was a fool's approach. If they were anything like Gafino, they would have men watching his every move.

"Who is it?"

"A guy by the name of Tex." He shook his head. "He runs a meth lab in Covington."

"That's where you live?"

"Yeah." He nodded looking despondent.

Jack wasn't sure whether to believe him or not. Though he couldn't help think that Billy was like him in some way. Perhaps, he was just someone looking to escape his past.

"Can you get me in contact with him?"

Billy frowned and then chuckled. "Are you kidding? If he even knows that I have told anyone about him, I'll be dead before the day is over. And besides you don't find him, he finds you. I have never dealt with him direct. Just his men."

"Then let's go pay them a visit."

"Are you out of your mind? I'm not going anywhere."

Jack stepped in real close to him. "Your girl is laying in another room because of you. She was raped, beaten and had her daughter's life threatened because of you. You want to be responsible? You want your life back? Then you need to start listening."

"Look, I don't know who the hell you are, and I appreciate you being here for Theresa but this is my family. And I will decide what is best. I will take care of this."

He brushed past Jack and left the room. Jack could have told him about Ruby but perhaps he knew. He could have slapped him around but it wouldn't have helped. He took a deep breath and exhaled hard before leaving the room and going back to where Theresa was. Billy hadn't even returned to her room. Billy was scared and didn't know what to do. It was a bad combination.

When Jack came back in, Theresa still looked

concerned.

"Jack, I need you to keep an eye on Ruby."

"She's with a friend, at least that's what Billy said."

She shook her head slightly. "I don't trust him, Jack."

"And you trust me?"

She cocked her head slightly before groaning.

Did she even know what Billy had got her involved in? He wanted to tell her, if only for Ruby's sake. Everyone was entitled to a second chance but now if he told her what Billy had got himself into, there was a chance she'd walk away. He hadn't decided if that was a good thing or not. He didn't know Billy, only his past and if the past determined the future, could anyone be trusted? Everyone in the world was marred in some way by those they had crossed paths with, for some, more than others.

"Give me the address of your place. You need to rest up. I'll look into this."

He didn't want to make any promises. He had no idea what he was up against except what Billy had told him, and he wasn't exactly convinced by anything that had come out of his mouth. There was the slim possibility that he was still caught up in it. That this had been the result of a deal gone wrong, or maybe he had attempted to flex his muscles and branch out on his own. It was common in the world where drugs and money flowed like milk and honey. A little bit off the top, a little bit of distribution over here without the head guy knowing and before long word gets back and they are staring down the barrel of a gun.

Before he left, Theresa reached out for Jack's hand. She ran her thumb over the back of his hand. She hesitated before speaking.

"Do you think things might have worked out between us if I had told you about being pregnant?"

"Maybe."

He stared at her and tried to remember what they were like. He'd often wondered what had become of her. At times he'd regretted choosing Gafino over her. But he didn't know any better back then. The crime syndicate had their claws deep inside him. Only those who had been a part of that lifestyle would understand. It was like coming out of prison after thirty years. People became institutionalized, and while logically they knew that freedom was not found behind bars, they got used to it. It became an inmate's world. Crime was like syrup that stuck to your fingers. Once in, it was very hard to get out without having it affect who you were. Looking at Billy was like looking at a younger version of himself. He was stubborn, didn't want to listen and thought he could figure it all out by himself. He respected that.

"Jack," she paused. "Don't let anything happen to her."

"You have my word."

He could see the pain in her eyes, the thought of Ruby being hurt far outweighed what she had gone through.

Jack left the hospital that day feeling as though he had just come out of surgery. His head was in a fog, his mind preoccupied with Theresa and his chest felt heavy from the weight of being told that he had a daughter.

He glanced down at the photo Theresa had given him,

trying to see the resemblance. The thought of harm coming to her was worse than any guilt he carried. He couldn't walk away. He wouldn't do it. Eddie had been there for him. How many times had he helped him at the expense of risking his own life? Jack felt a sense of anger in the pit of his stomach.

Right then his phone rang. He looked down and saw that it was Judith calling.

Shit! He had completely forgotten. They were meant to meet over an hour ago.

He tapped accept and put the phone up to his ear.

"I'm sorry, something came up."

She wanted to know if they could reschedule for the evening. He agreed to meet her just after five. He hung up and looked up to see the taxi still waiting there. Jamaican music blared out of the speakers and Jamaar was grinning while smoking what looked like a joint. He didn't want to even think about how much he owed him. He slipped in and gave him the address in Covington.

"You know this is going to cost you a pretty packet."

Jack glanced at the meter.

"Looks like it already has."

As the taxi rumbled away, he leaned back and looked out the window before glancing at the photo of his daughter Ruby.

Chapter 11

Isabel had arrived the previous evening. For the better part of the morning she had been down at the main New Orleans police station relaying information on Jack Winchester. In many ways it was kind of useless as they seemed overwhelmed by the approaching storm and short-handed on officers.

"Look, I'm not asking you to dedicate an entire task force to this. I just need to have your men keep an eye out for this man."

She handed him a sheet of paper with Jack Winchester's mug shot. The overweight officer groaned as he looked at it. Everything about her exchange with him felt as though she was pulling teeth. Anyone would have thought she was asking him to do a hundred jumping jacks. She glanced at his belly that hung over his utility belt and shook her head.

"Shaun, run off a few copies of this and hand them out

to some of the guys. Also send over the details to those on patrol." He looked back at Isabel. "Happy?"

"Thank you," she said before turning and walking over to the coffee machine. She pulled out the murky glass carafe and sloshed around what remained in the bottom. She brought it up to her nostrils and winced at the smell. How long had that been there? Did they ever change it? One look inside the filter and the green mold on top of the coffee grounds answered that.

"They haven't changed it in over a month. There is a coffee store half a block down from us now. They all go there."

Isabel nodded to the woman officer jabbing at a keyboard. She checked her phone to see if Cooper had managed to get the address of Theresa Rizzo. There was nothing. She shot him a quick text telling him to speed it up. At the rate he was going Jack would be long gone. She didn't expect him to stick around — if he was even in New Orleans.

It was possible that Detective Banfield's death had

been a mob hit. His involvement in bringing down the Sicilian cartel would have sent shock waves throughout the crime syndicate families. Payback would have been a given. It wouldn't have been the first time that the FBI had been called in to clean up after the mob had taken out officers and lawyers involved in putting away key figures. That was the danger that came with the job.

Her phone vibrated and she glanced down. It was Cooper.

Sorry, I had to go in to get medically cleared. They won't clear me for field work. Can you believe that? Here's the address for her workplace. Call me when you get a chance. I'm trying to fight them on this but Simon is being an asshole.

She couldn't help feel a smidgen of guilt over their decision. Ultimately it did come down to whether or not they felt he was physically ready to deal with fieldwork again. It wasn't just about whether he could hold a gun, or fight his way out of a situation. They also tested you mentally to make sure you wouldn't fly off the handle.

Isabel didn't wait around a minute longer.

* * *

Inside the hotel it was busy. For someone who had ties to the mob, the work didn't exactly fit what she imagined a former stripper would do. She figured it would have been a dilapidated old motel with bed bugs and roaches crawling across the floor. Theresa had certainly gone up in the world.

She waited patiently behind a group of tourists from Ireland. They had obviously been drinking already. All of them were holding go-cups and they all smelled to high heaven of liquor.

"I want to be upgraded to a better suite. That suite you have us in is shit. There are wires hanging out of the air conditioning unit and water on the floor. This is supposed to be a five-star hotel. I hope you are going to give us a better deal. Perhaps you can take some money off our bill?"

Isabel tapped her foot hoping this wasn't going to take too long.

"We are very sorry. We'll have you changed over to another room immediately."

"Yes, yes you will."

She stifled a laugh. It never ceased to amaze her how rude people could be when it came to travel. It was as if they expected to be treated like gold. Sure, they needed to be moved but they could have dropped the attitude. Since walking in she hadn't seen anything that would suggest this place wasn't up to standard. The floors were gleaming, there was a cleaner polishing the buttons on the elevator. There was free coffee and WiFi, comfy chairs to sit in and the small store on the first floor had a sign that read: FREE toothbrushes and toothpaste, just in case you forgot.

Even as the clerk tried his best to deescalate the situation by promising to have them changed over to another room, they still didn't let up. Filled with liquid courage, they were starting to become belligerent. Isabel slipped up beside them and pulled out her badge.

"I need a word with you."

The clerk gestured to her to come around the side.

"What the hell? We've been waiting here ages and you just barge in front of the line."

"Take a seat and cool off," Isabel said as she came around the side. They cursed at her but she just ignored it. The clerk let her through a locked side door and she followed him into the back room. He looked nervous.

"What's this about?"

"I'm trying to track down an employee of yours by the name of Theresa Rizzo."

"You are the second person that has been in asking about her. What is this all about?"

"Second?"

Outside the door the guests were getting even louder. One of them had decided he wanted his money back. They weren't going to stay another minute in the hotel and demanded an immediate refund.

"Yeah," he replied, meanwhile casting a nervous glance

around her.

"Male, female?"

"Male."

"Can you describe him?"

"About six foot, well built, dark hair, white."

It could have been any number of people. Isabel fished inside her suit jacket and pulled out a folded piece of paper with a mug shot of Jack. She handed it to him.

"Is this the guy?"

"That's him. Yeah, without a doubt."

"When was he here?"

"Maybe a few hours ago."

Isabel felt her pulse race a little.

"What did he want?"

"The same thing as you. He wanted to know where Theresa was. I told him she was over at New Orleans East Hospital."

She frowned. "Why?"

"I haven't a clue. We received a phone call from a friend of hers to say she had an accident."

"Do you have a pen?"

The man looked around the room and pulled out a pen from a desk drawer. Isabel turned over the mug shot and scribbled her cell number on it.

"Call me if he shows up again."

The clerk nodded and she made her way back out. By now the Irish tourists looked as if they were going to destroy some of the property if they didn't get their money back. Isabel was about to leave when she walked up to the loudest guy and told him to show some manners.

"This guy works hard. Probably holds down two jobs. Yelling isn't going to get you that refund any quicker. So take a seat. Let him do his job and you can be on your way."

"Get lost."

He shoved Isabel as he tried to make his way back to the counter. Isabel grabbed a hold of his arm and twisted it around until the guy dropped to one knee in agony. The other guy and two women who were with him started protesting.

"You are hurting him. Let him go."

"Back off."

"Now that wasn't smart. You know it's an offense to assault an FBI agent?"

His eyes bulged. She let him go. "Now go take a seat."

As he shuffled back to his seat, his wife, or girlfriend tried to console him. That only angered him even more. He glared at Isabel as she walked out. Some things never changed. It had been a while since she had to get all up in someone's face. It reminded her of her days on the force. She couldn't count the number of nights she was called out to a drunken brawl. Those were some of the highlights of her career. She had the battle scars to show for it too. A scar on the right of her abdomen and a scar behind her ear were all a reminder of why she didn't miss it.

Chapter 12

Fairland trailer park was located on the east side of Covington. The taxi pulled in and Jack handed Jamaar some cash to cover the trip.

"You want me to stick around, mon?"

"No, I should be good now."

"Well, you know where I am if you need me. Here's my card."

He fumbled around inside the glove compartment and retrieved a business card. Jack looked at it. It was for some strip joint in the area. On the back was his number with the words *Have a nice day* scribbled across the top.

Jack frowned, looked at Jamaar and he started laughing. "Day or night, I don't sleep much. Give me a shout."

Jack shook his hand and the odd-looking taxi pulled away playing reggae music. A couple of neighbors sat in armchairs out the front drinking beer. They eyed him skeptically, he gave a nod but they didn't return it. A few steps and he knocked on a door. He could hear someone inside rushing around. He backed up and it creaked open.

Ruby looked out.

"Carla, it's some man."

Whoever was caring for her must have not heard, as they never responded. Jack looked at her and smiled. "You must be Ruby?"

"That's right. How did you know that?"

"Magic."

"Show us a trick."

He crouched down in front of her and he did the old pull your finger off gimmick. She grinned and shook her head.

"You're just folding over your finger."

"Smart kid."

She stepped out and took a seat on the concrete steps that led up into the trailer. From inside the smell of cooked sausages wafted out.

"Who's Carla?"

"She's a friend of my mom. Have you seen my mom?"

"Yeah. Yeah I have."

"Where is she?"

"She's visiting family but she told me to let you know that she will be back in a couple of days."

"Do you want to see my bike?"

"Um," he looked at the door again wondering if this Carla girl was going to come out. "Maybe in a minute. I just want to check in on your friend."

Jack knocked a few more times on the door but there was no answer.

"She's sleeping," Ruby replied. Jack pulled on the door handle and went inside. He cast his gaze over the state of the place. It was a shithole. Dishes lined the counter and filled the sink. The floor looked as if it hadn't seen a vacuum cleaner and the curtains were yellow from smoke. As he walked back through the cramped living room area and passed the kitchen into the place where the beds were, he saw a young girl with dark hair laid out on a bed with a glass pipe beside her. He picked it up and smelled it. It was meth.

Ruby came running up from behind him.

"Hey, why don't you go play outside for a bit? I just want to have a word with Carla."

Ruby nodded and shot off. He couldn't believe Theresa would let her live in this state. It was disgusting. These weren't conditions fit for any child. How could anyone allow this? He leaned over the girl and shook her a little. She groaned and muttered something that sounded as if she was telling Ruby to go away. Jack gave her another shake and her eyelids popped open. They widened fast and she let out a scream. He immediately put his hand over her mouth. She bit it and shoved him back. Like someone being jolted with an electrical shock, she bolted upright and was about to dart down the narrow hallway when Jack caught her leg and she tripped. She gasped as she landed hard against the floor.

When he finally managed to get control of her and she promised not to scream, he released his hand from her mouth.

"I'm a friend of Theresa's. Jack Winchester."

"Jack?" Her eyes scanned the floor as if trying to process or remember what Theresa might have told her. "I don't know you."

"Well, phone her and you'll see."

He took a seat on the bed and waited as Carla made the call. He made sure she wasn't going to dash off by closing the door that separated the corridor from the bedroom. A few minutes later she hung up.

"The baby daddy."

"She's not exactly a baby anymore."

Carla folded her arms across her chest and leaned back against the wall of the trailer. She blew out her cheeks then reached for a packet of cigarettes on the side table.

"You think getting high when you're supposed to be looking after a kid is smart?"

"She's old enough to take care of herself. I just said to Theresa I would keep an eye on her."

She blew out a puff of smoke and Jack fanned the air with his hand. "You want one?"

He shook his head. "Trying to give them up." He looked around. "If this is her room, where's Ruby's?"

She grinned. "This isn't Theresa's place. Oh no, she lives down on Wellington Drive. This is Billy's. He lets me stay here."

That was a relief.

"What number?"

"Sixty-two."

Jack rose up from the bed and walked back out into the living room area. The whole place made him feel down. He sighed heavily. "How long have you been on that stuff?"

"Two years."

He looked at her face. She was beginning to show signs of meth usage. Her teeth were decaying, she was suffering from hair loss and her skin had a few open sores. It was sick to look at. Why anyone would pump their body with that crap was incomprehensible. Jack picked up a pipe that was on a side table.

"You do know there's chemicals and shit in this," he

said.

She lifted up a cigarette between her two yellowed fingers. "So? There is in this, and it doesn't make me feel as half as good as meth does." She gave a toothy grin and took a seat at the table. She was wearing a skimpy stained top with no bra, and a pair of cut-off jean shorts. On the table in front of her was an ashtray that hadn't been emptied in god knows when. She picked up a cup that looked as if it had cold coffee in it and downed it. He grimaced.

"Listen, I can look after Ruby for now."

"You can?" She almost sounded relieved. Probably wanted to get back to her pipe. Within seconds she was up and gathering together Ruby's bag. It was a backpack that was partially open. Inside were coloring books and a soft bear. Jack shook his head at the thought of her life. Kids had no idea. All they wanted was to be loved. He knew by the way Theresa talked about her, that she cared deeply for her daughter. But it was Billy that worried him.

Carla handed off keys to him.

"It's a red brick house, number sixty-two."

She tapped her cigarette again on the side table and ash scattered. He was going to tell her to use an ashtray but he didn't bother.

"Thanks."

He let himself out. Outside Ruby was riding around on a red bike that had tassels that hung off the handles. She honked the horn and smiled, completely oblivious to the dismal life that surrounded her. In some ways that was a good thing.

"You ready to go?"

Her eyes darted to Jack and then Carla.

"He's going to take you home. Go on now."

Chapter 13

Sixty-two Wellington Drive was three blocks from the trailer park. Along the way Jack couldn't take his eyes off Ruby. The knowledge that she was his child hadn't fully sunk in. He already regretted most of his life choices but now he felt a wave of shame. He wasn't father material. With the FBI breathing down his neck, he knew he wouldn't be able to stay in Louisiana long. Life on the road for a kid was no life. Besides, he'd been out of her life for eight years. She probably thought Billy was her father. He'd forgotten to ask Theresa about that.

Ruby circled her bike around him as they got closer to her home. She hadn't stopped yakking since leaving the trailer park. At one time it would have been annoying but there was something different about it when it came from your own kid. It amused him.

"Why have I never seen you and mom together?"

"What do you mean?"

"You are her friend, yes?"

He nodded and his lip curled up, finding her question amusing.

"But I've never seen you. Friends hang out together."

"Ah, yeah, well, I've been away."

"On vacation?"

"Something like that."

Right then an ice cream truck jingled a tune that would attract kids in the area. It stopped one block down from where they were.

"You want an ice cream?"

"Really?"

"Yeah, why not."

A few minutes later they approached her house. Ruby had ice cream around her lips and a big smile on her face. It was a red brick house with a front yard that looked as if it hadn't seen a lawn mower in several months. Overgrown and with several large bald cypress and maple trees out the front that provided a lot of shade from the heat of the day. They hadn't made it within a few feet of the door when Billy came out.

"What are you doing with Ruby?"

"Bringing her home."

He motioned with his head. "Go on inside."

"But I…"

"Get inside," he yelled. Ruby dashed in without hesitation. No doubt this hadn't been the first time he yelled at her. Jack clenched his jaw. Though he'd been told he was her biological father, he didn't know for sure and he'd been out of the picture too long to say anything. Now if Billy swatted her, it might have been a different case. Billy closed the door behind him so she couldn't hear the conversation he was about to have. He stepped out into the yard.

"I don't know who you are, or what you are up to but I think it's time you moved on."

Jack noticed that he was twitching and scratching at his arm. He noticed a few sores.

"You taking meth?"

"What the hell's it to do with you?"

"Did you arrange for me to speak to one of Tex's guys?"

"I told you. I'm going to handle business."

"And if you can't? What happens to Ruby? To Theresa?"

"Get the fuck out of here."

Jack balled his fist then looked over his shoulder when he saw movement. Ruby was at the door peeking out. A part of him wanted to put Billy on his ass but he wouldn't do it with her watching. Jack was still carrying Ruby's bag. He handed it off to Billy. Billy snatched it from his hand, making it clear he disliked him. Regardless of whether Billy was on meth or not, he could understand not wanting another guy around, especially one he'd never met before. Jack turned around and began walking away. The door banged shut behind him and he paused for a second, listening to make sure that Billy wasn't taking out his frustration on Ruby. Satisfied, he turned back toward the road. He'd only made it a few feet when he heard feet coming up behind him. That's when he felt a soft hand reach for his. He looked back and saw the door was wide open and Ruby was holding his hand.

"Thanks for the ice cream."

He nodded, and his lip curled up.

With that she let go and ran back inside. He stood there for a few more seconds and then continued on his way.

* * *

When Isabel arrived at the hospital she didn't expect to see Theresa so badly beaten. She was sleeping when she came into the room. Isabel took a seat in a chair across from her and studied her face. Had Jack done this?

Over the course of an hour she drank two cups of coffee and waited for her to wake. When she began to stir, Isabel sat upright and smoothed out her suit that had become wrinkled from dozing off.

"Who are you?" Theresa muttered.

She took out her badge and flashed it. "I'm Agent Baker, I was hoping to have a few words with you about Jack Winchester."

Theresa chuckled a little.

"What's funny?"

"Not much has changed."

"You knew him back when he was in New York?"

"That I did."

"What happened, Theresa? Was it him?"

"Jack?" she snorted a little and then groaned in pain. "Jack would never harm me. He would never harm any woman."

"He has a rap sheet a mile long. I find it hard to believe that."

"Then you don't know him."

"Maybe you can fill me in."

"What are you here for?" Theresa asked in a tone that made it clear that she was averse to being grilled by the FBI.

"After Jack got out of prison, numerous members of the New York Mafia were killed. A year later, key figures in the Sicilian family were murdered. A month ago, he not only killed several Triad gang members but we believe he is responsible for the death of several other men. I'm here to bring him in."

"Whatever they did, they probably had it coming."

"How so?"

"Jack might have run with the wrong crowd when he was younger but he's not a cold-blooded killer."

Isabel stifled a laugh. It was always the same with criminals. Women stood by their men no matter what. They could always see the good in them and never the bad. Whatever they did was justified in their eyes.

"The trail of blood that he has left behind him paints a very different picture of him."

"I don't know what you have seen but whoever forced his hand had a choice."

"So did Jack before he killed them. Theresa, justifying his actions isn't doing anyone any favors. Murder is murder no matter how you try to spin it."

"I don't have anything to say to you."

Isabel shook her head in disbelief.

"Did he do this to you?"

"I told you, it wasn't Jack."

"Have you seen him?"

She didn't reply.

"Theresa, I know he was here. Your work told me. Now all you are doing is preventing me from doing my job."

Again she didn't say anything.

"You have a child?"

Theresa's eyes looked in Isabel's direction before glancing away. She had no idea if she had a child but usually the mention of one would drive home the point she was trying to make. Those who didn't would tell you straight away, those who did would get defensive or go real quiet. Isabel knew she wasn't going to get any more out of her. She needed to let her sit with the questions. Sometimes it just required little bit of time to ponder what might happen if they didn't cooperate.

She rose to her feet and ferreted inside her jacket for a card. She placed it on the bedside table.

"When you want to talk, phone me. I'm staying at the

Crowne Plaza. Room 401."

Theresa glanced over at the card and Isabel left the room.

* * *

Jack slumped down on his bed in his hotel room with a glass of bourbon. He didn't consider himself a heavy drinker. The years of getting lost at the bottom of a bottle were behind him. It clouded his thinking, caused him to make rash decisions and at times just made him not want to do anything. Thankfully, even the smallest amount, as of late, gave him headaches. As he sipped at his drink he pulled out the crinkled photo of Ruby and stared at her. He placed it on the side table and then went to the balcony. From his room he could hear and see what was going on down on Bourbon Street. At night it was lit up and the sound of music seeping out of bars filled the air. Tourists crowded the streets with laughter, chatter and the occasional fight. Neon signs illuminated the night as Jack leaned against the iron railing. The temperature had dropped considerably since the afternoon, a harsh coastal wind had made its way in and thunder could be heard rumbling in the distance. Behind him the TV was on. The volume was low, barely audible. Jack went back inside and flipped through the channels until he reached the weather channel.

Hurricane warnings flashed across the screen. At this point they were just advising people to be prepared. Jack turned it off and chuckled. It didn't matter what the media said, people would still do whatever the hell they liked, especially tourists who had come down here to have a good time.

Jack's phone began buzzing. He looked down at the caller ID and saw it was Theresa. When he answered she sounded slightly panicked.

"An FBI agent came in to see me tonight."

"Who were they?"

"There was just one. A female by the name of Agent Baker."

Jack stepped out on the balcony with the phone against his ear. She'd found him.

He sighed. "What did you tell her?"

"Nothing. You know me."

That was one thing he could count on. Theresa had never been the kind of woman that turned on anyone. It just wasn't in her DNA. She had distaste for the law. He never quite knew why. Perhaps it was because of her frequent run-ins she'd had when she worked at the strip joint

"What have you got yourself into?"

Jack sucked air between his teeth

"Eddie is dead."

"What? When did that happen?"

"Long story, I'll fill you in when I see you. I don't know how secure this line is."

"Jack, I thought you had finally got away from it all."

"I have. I mean… I had. I'm no longer associated with any of the families in New York. I'm trying to start again but, you know how things go. Trouble always seems to find me and walking away from it, well…" He looked at a group of guys with beads around their necks. They had got the season completely wrong. Mardi Gras was in February. They were shouting up at empty open windows asking for women to show their breasts.

"What's all that yelling?"

Jack walked back inside but didn't reply.

"Where did the agent go?"

"I don't know, she left me a card. She's staying at the Crowne Plaza."

"Did she give a room number?"

"401."

Jack nodded slowly, contemplating what to do. Logic told him to pack his things and get the hell out of there. But with Billy having pissed off the wrong people, the thought of leaving without knowing that Theresa and Ruby were safe wasn't something he could handle. He had to stay.

"Right. Thanks, Theresa."

"Did you see Ruby today?" she asked.

He chuckled a little. "Yeah, she's a real firecracker."

She stifled a laugh. "That she is. She has your eyes,

Jack."

"And your face. She's beautiful."

There was silence on the other end. "I didn't mean…"

"No, it's okay."

"Look, I want to help but I can't force my way into this. Billy has his back up with me being around."

"Leave him to me. I'll speak to him this evening."

"Theresa. You know he's using."

She didn't reply immediately. "Yeah, I kind of figured."

"Whatever he's got himself involved in, they aren't just going to walk away. What they did to you is just the beginning to what they will do if…"

"If?"

There was no easy way to tell her. He just came out with it.

"Billy owes someone forty thousand dollars. If they don't get it within forty-eight hours, then…"

He heard her curse on the other end of the line.

"Why don't you just take Ruby and get away from

here?"

"Because I love him, Jack. I want to kill him most days, but when he's not on that shit, he's… He's been off it for a year. I can't believe he's taking it again."

"Stress will do that."

"So will stupidity," she replied.

Despite her sordid past, Theresa had never touched drugs. In many ways she was a lot like Jack. She liked her drink but that was it. She drew the line at drugs.

"I'll speak to him. He listens to me."

"Right."

Jack hung up and sprawled out on his bed. His thoughts circled around his daughter, Agent Baker and the situation that was looming over them. There wasn't going to be an easy way out of this. No matter what he did, someone was going to get hurt.

Chapter 14

The information for her place of work arrived in his phone in the early hours of the morning. Giovanni had arrived in New Orleans on a flight from New York sometime in the middle of the afternoon. He had booked into a hotel located down on Frenchmen Street. He'd been waiting for his contact to meet him and growing impatient with every minute that passed.

Eventually there was a knock at the door. He went over and peeked through the peephole. Outside a small guy with a grey suit on, white shirt and no tie looked around nervously. He tapped again. Giovanni cracked the door open and the guy mentioned Salvatore. He let him in and glanced up and down the corridor before closing the door behind him.

"What was the delay?"

"Sorry, my supplier wasn't available. I ended up going with another one and he was running late." The guy talked as he walked around. "They got a mini bar in here?"

He pulled open the fridge and Giovanni closed it.

"Do you have it?"

"Yeah."

He slapped down on the bed a large case. Unzipping the bag, he flipped it back to reveal two Glock G17 pistols, a Marlin 1894 CB .45 Colt and several other handguns with suppressors.

"Take your pick."

Giovanni picked up a Glock, slapped a magazine in it and loaded a round.

"Hey, hey, what are you doing?"

He glanced at the man before pointing it at him.

"How's it look?"

The guy put up his hands. "Shit, dude, put it down."

He released the magazine and pulled the slider back to pop out the one in the chamber.

"I'll take it."

"And the rifle?"

"Leave it all."

"You got cash?"

"Salvatore is handling it."

"No, no. I'm only taking cash. The last time I dealt with him I told him that the next time I got paid, I received green. I'm not messing around here."

He placed the Glock back in with the other one and proceeded to zip up the bag.

"Leave the bag."

"No, fuck that, if you don't have the green, we're done."

While the man was zipping up the bag, Giovanni slowly pulled out metal wire from the back of his ring. It was coiled inside. The man was bent over at the hip and was griping about being ripped off and having people waste his time when Giovanni looped the wire around his neck and tugged hard. Both of them fell back on the ground and the man's face went a deep red as he continued pulling hard. He reached up and tried to grab Giovanni's hair but he just turned his head so it was out of reach. Choking and gasping for air he tried to pry loose the wire but it was useless. His legs smashed hard against the bed and they slid back on the smooth floor until Giovanni no longer felt any resistance. He remained there for a few more minutes holding the same amount of tension. There were always the ones that went unconscious. It wasn't worth taking chances. He kept pulling on the wire until it cut deep into his throat. No sound came from the man and he knew he was dead.

Satisfied, he rolled him off his body and dragged him into the bathroom. He placed his body in the bath, tore down the shower curtain and laid it over him. It wasn't done as an act of respect, he just didn't want to stare at his grotesque face.

He shook his head. They never learned.

Returning to his room, he flipped through the phone for the address of Theresa Rizzo's workplace. It was a block down from him. He adjusted his tie in the mirror and smoothed out his suit. On the floor, the guy's phone was laying just under the bed. He picked it up and wiped it off. After, he tossed it in with the body before retrieving the two Glocks. He removed his suit jacket, slipped into the gun harness and placed one either side.

It was early morning when he left, though it didn't appear that way when he stepped outside. It was dark. This was the city that never slept. He slipped down the street barely noticed by the passersby gawking at the strip joints and bars. Some drunk asked him for some money but he ignored him. When he arrived at the hotel he stepped inside, glanced around at the empty lobby, locked the double doors behind him and approached the side of the desk. His eyes drifted around the room looking for security cameras. They were there. They always were. Every hotel was different, some would have them in full sight, and others were hidden. In this case they were hidden. He went up to the door and banged on the side.

"Can I help you?"

A voice bellowed from out back, as there was no one at the front desk. They were probably sitting watching TV. It was rare to find any clerk at the desk in the early hours of the morning. He came around, pulled his gun and hopped over the counter.

"That you can."

The man's eyes flared in horror as he grabbed hold of him and forced him back into a small office.

"First, where are the recordings for the surveillance?"

The man pointed to the corner. Down below was a small black machine with lights that flickered. Giovanni yanked it out, cables and all.

"Any others?"

The man shook his head, scared out of his mind.

"Where can I find Theresa Rizzo?"

"Is this a joke?"

"Does it look like I'm joking?"

The man reached for a drawer and Giovanni gave him a look.

"Two other people have been in. She's in the East Hospital."

Giovanni stared at him blankly. He still had a firm grip on him as he pulled out his phone, flicked through for a photo of Jack Winchester.

"Was this one of them?"

"Yeah."

"And the other?"

"FBI."

He nodded thoughtfully.

The man raised his hands. "Please. I have a kid and wife."

"That's nice. So did I."

With that he stepped back a few paces, raised the Glock and fired one round into the man's forehead. He took the recording device with him and exited the hotel. Outside, no one paid attention as he slipped unnoticed into a cluster of tourists.

Chapter 15

By early morning, as a deep orange sun peeked over the horizon, Jack had already been up several hours. He sat inside the lobby of the Crowne Plaza wearing a baseball cap, shades and reading a paper. He hadn't slept much that night. The thought of the FBI coming after him had unnerved him. Why were they going to this much trouble? Why hadn't U.S. Marshals been sent in to get him? He had a lot of questions and needed answers. He'd waited in the lobby for the better part of an hour, hoping to see her come down for breakfast. Sure enough, just a little after seven-thirty in the morning, she shuffled out of an elevator. He held the paper up as she passed by not even looking at him or the other three people who were talking among themselves.

Already knowing what room she was in, he watched her from a distance. As soon as he saw that she was at the breakfast buffet he slipped into the elevator and went up to the third floor. Moving fast, he noticed several maids going in and out of rooms.

"Excuse me. I've got locked out of my room. Stupid. I left the key card inside. Would you mind?"

The young girl looked at him. "I'm really not supposed to."

He flashed her his best smile. "I'd get my wife but she's already left for the day."

"I will radio down to front desk."

He pointed to the card on the chain around her waist.

"But it would be so much quicker if you just…"

She struggled with the decision. All the while Jack's pulse was racing. He knew he didn't have long. He just need to get an idea of what was going on with this FBI agent.

"Okay. Which room is it?"

He led her down to the door and she let him in.

"You are an angel and did anyone ever tell you, you have a lovely smile."

She wandered off grinning from ear to ear. As the door

closed behind him he looked around for her luggage. On a side table was her phone. He picked it up and tried to access it but there was a lock on it. Damn! He placed it back down and started rooting through her luggage. She had quite a taste for thongs, he chuckled to himself and tossed them back down. Nothing.

That's when he noticed on the table a leather folder. He unzipped it and flipped it open. Inside, staring back at him was his mug shot. *What the heck?* All these details were listed below it. He browsed through the other paperwork that had an FBI logo at the top. There was information from the L.A. police department. It had his rap sheet and a piece of paper with Dana Grant's name, address and phone number. *Dana.* Jack grabbed a notepad, and jotted it down. He tore off the paper and pocketed it. He continued rooting through her things until he heard the lock on the door. He pulled his piece and watched as the door handle went down. Then, just as he thought he was about to come face-to-face with her, the door closed. Not wasting anytime he rushed up to the door and peered out the peephole. She was speaking with a woman across from her. *Shit! Think, think.*

His eyes scanned the room. He saw the closet. *No, stupid.*

He rushed over to the window and opened the double doors that led out to the balcony. He closed them behind him and cautiously stepped over the edge on to the side of the ledge. The wind whipped around him. A light rain was beginning to fall making the stone slippery. It wasn't very wide at all. He grimaced as he edged his way out. He hated heights, that and water. Shuffling along he moved over to the next balcony and hopped over. He checked the doors but they were locked. Right then he heard doors open. He squeezed himself back as hard as he could against the door of the room next to hers.

There was a small wall that jutted out and divided the two rooms. He took a deep breath and then…

Just when he was about to step back out, the doors behind him opened and he fell backwards into the room landing hard on top of the guest. He was a fat businessman who immediately started cursing. Jack rolled over and placed his hand over the guy's mouth.

"Shut up."

He wouldn't listen so Jack pulled out his Glock and placed it against the side of his head. That soon shut him up. He dragged him up and pulled him into the washroom. Using the tie from the bathrobe he tied the guy's hands to the towel rack and shoved a washcloth into his mouth.

"Sorry about this."

He backed out of the bathroom and cracked open the door to the corridor. Peeking out, he saw there was no one there except the maid carts. He placed a DO NOT DISTURB sign on the door handle before he exited. Not wasting another second he darted out and double-timed it down the corridor, shouldered the fire escape door and took the stairs two at a time. Within a matter of minutes, he was on the ground floor.

* * *

Isabel was relieved to pull herself away from the

woman across the hall who she'd met on the way in. She was a single woman, traveling on business and obviously in desperate need of company as any time Isabel opened the door, she'd open hers. It made her wonder if she was sitting at the peephole checking on her comings and goings. It was very odd.

A light breeze blew in through the window. She stepped back inside and noticed something that wasn't there before. Her folder was open. It wasn't zipped up fully, a piece of paper was sticking out the side. Her eyes went to her phone, then to her luggage. Sure enough it had been moved. Her first thoughts were the maid had been in and had been rooting around. She went over to the door and stepped outside. Looking up and down she saw a maid cart six rooms down. As she was strolling down to it, the maid came out.

"Um, have you been in my room yet?"

"No, I have these rooms to do before I get to yours."

"Strange. Some of my belongings looked out of place."

"Probably your husband."

"Husband?"

"Yeah, he asked me to let him in."

A cold shiver ran through her as she reached for her piece. The maid screamed. Moving fast she went back to the room and entered with her gun in her outstretched hands. The first thing she checked was the closet that was closed. She slid back the door and breathed out hard. Her heart was pounding in her chest as she moved through the room checking until she was out on the balcony. She glanced to her right, then her left. That's when she saw a footprint on the concrete. Dirt had mixed in with it to leave a clear print.

Bolting out of the room she began banging on the next door. When there was no answer she had the maid let her in. As soon as she was inside she caught the reflection of the guest tied to the towel rack in the washroom. She went in and untied him, pulled the wash cloth out.

"Where is he?"

"He left, five minutes ago."

She didn't hang around to listen to the rest of the rant.

Isabel dashed out of the room and raced down the corridor to the stairs. She nearly stumbled on her way down. She couldn't believe it. He'd been in her room. She'd been this close to nabbing him again. Anger gripped her as she kept her gun low and padded down the stairs. At the bottom she burst through the door into the lobby. A few guests shrieked at the sight of the gun.

"FBI," she yelled to try and alleviate their fears, not that it helped.

She dashed outside onto the sidewalk and looked up and down the crowd of people. Her eyes scanned the faces for Jack Winchester, but he was gone. Disappeared again.

"Shit!" she yelled.

Chapter 16

Billy Dixon pulled up in front of the home of Mike Oakley. He was an old friend, both of them had worked together distributing meth long before he went inside and long before he had got involved with Tex. Mike owed him a favor and now it was time to repay. He banged on the door and from inside a guy yelled.

"Hang on, hang on."

A few seconds passed and the door opened. Billy brushed past him not even asking to be let in.

"Billy, what the hell? I thought you was banged up."

"I was."

He went into his kitchen and paced around. He was twitching like crazy and scratching at his neck. It felt as if something was crawling under his skin.

"You got any?"

He snorted. "Dude, you need to get off that shit."

"Just hook me up. I need to talk to you about a few

things."

Mike frowned. "Follow me."

He led him through into a living area that had a giant LED TV on the wall and thick, black leather sofas. On the coffee table in full view were packets of pale blue meth and a few pipes.

"Help yourself. This is the good shit."

"Listen, I need you to do me a big one."

Mike sank back into one of his chairs. His dreadlocks hung down loosely over his face as he lit a cigar and blew out a large cloud of grey smoke.

"I don't owe you anything."

"The hell you do. Or have you forgotten that I bailed you out of that deal that went bad? That was ten grand."

"So what, you want ten grand?"

"Forty."

"What the hell?"

He sat forward in his chair with the cigar resting between his fingers.

"Call it interest."

"Interest? Get the hell out of my place."

"Look, I have twenty-four hours left to pay this off or I'm screwed."

Mike stared back at him with a look of confusion. "Who the hell have you pissed off?"

Billy snorted up some of the meth. For a moment his body shook and his eyes rolled back inside his skull, then he got this wild look in his eyes as if his internal battery had just been recharged. He pulled at his nostrils and rested back on the sofa before lighting a cigarette.

"Damn, that is some fine shit."

Billy's phone buzzed, he took it out and saw that it was Theresa. He ignored it and placed it on the table.

"Only the best."

"You have to be careful. Tex finds out that you're dealing, he will bring the hammer down on you."

"Screw Tex. Guy is full of himself. He can't corner the market. There is more than enough room."

Billy stared back at him blankly.

"It's Tex, isn't it?" Mike asked.

He nodded.

Mike brought a fist up to his mouth and sucked in air between his teeth. "Crap, man. I want to help you, but forty G's? Business is good but not that good. I have to fly under the radar. If I was dealing in that kind of money, he would be all over me."

Billy took a hard pull on the cigarette. It glowed a bright orange at the end in the dimly lit room. He glanced around and got up. "How much meth you got on you?"

"Stacks, man, I just had my guy cook up a large batch that will take us through to next year. You got to see this."

Mike rose to his feet and shuffled into the next room, Billy followed. There was a pool table and a bar that had at least sixty bottles of alcohol. Mike went around the side of the bar and reached under it. There was a click and then a wall opened up across the room.

"Huh! What about that?"

"Slick."

Inside stacked in large clear bags was more than enough meth to put Mike away for the rest of his life. He went inside and picked up a bag and held it up to the light.

"Look how clear that is. My new guy is a genius. This is the purest you are ever going to see. Tex's stuff doesn't even come close to this. I have four guys who are producing this for me. They get forty percent; my take is sixty because I provide them with the ingredients."

"And you get that from who?"

"A supplier."

Billy snorted. "Are you sure that's not Tex?" Billy moved past him and tallied up in his head what he could get for this on the market. His pulse began racing fast. It was more than enough to cover him for what he owed and he could probably come out on top. The cogs in his mind began spinning at the thought of getting out of this situation. He had less than twenty-four hours to settle the score. He could pay back Tex, sell the rest and take Theresa and Ruby away from here. Mike was gloating over his stash when Billy jammed his gun against the back of Mike's head.

"What the hell are you doing?"

"Sorry, Mike, but I don't have a choice."

"I can give you the ten grand if that's what you want."

"It's not."

He knew Mike wouldn't have given him forty grand, let alone paid him back the ten. That was the nature of this business. People turned on each other fast and it didn't matter what history you had with others. It was all about the money, staying alive and coming out on top. He pulled the trigger and red mist sprayed back on his face before Mike collapsed on top of the goods. Moving fast, Billy started tossing the bags out. He rolled Mike off the remaining product. How do I get this out of here? His heart was pounding in his chest. The thought of being caught by any of Mike's guys was sending him into a mild panic attack. He raced upstairs and pulled a sheet off the king size bed. He would use it to create a makeshift sack. He laid it out downstairs and piled the hand-sized bags of meth into the middle of it, then folded up the sides and twisted the ends together. As he tried to pick it up about ten bags fell out. It weighed a ton. Then there was the body. *Ah screw him. I just need to get this out.* He could probably drag it out but it was going to look suspicious and who knew if anyone was watching. He was going to need a hand and at least four travel cases.

His mind was racing as he paced back and forth. Occasionally he glanced at Mike's corpse. Fuck! He didn't want to kill him but this called for extreme measures. *What was that guy's name? Joe? Jacob? Jack. Jack. That's it.* Maybe he could get him to help. He wanted to help. Now he could.

Chapter 17

Isabel was determined to get answers. She was tired of playing games. Arriving at the hospital that morning she had made a point to let the front desk know that she didn't want to get interrupted. When she opened the door to Theresa's room, Theresa was up and hobbling back to bed.

"We need to talk."

"I've told you what I know."

"Bullshit. Now you can keep lying and I can have you charged for assisting a known fugitive or you cut that crap and tell me where he is."

Theresa slipped back underneath the covers and raised up the back of the bed. Her face while still bruised looked slightly better than it had a day earlier. Isabel took a seat across from her and waited for her to speak.

"We used to see each other. Back in New York. I moved away from there eight years ago. I was pregnant with his kid," she said.

"Did he know?"

"No."

"Is he here because you told him?"

She shook her head. "No, I figured he must be in trouble. I used to help him where I could. I guess he must have wanted to reconnect. Maybe get back together?"

"And are you?"

"No, I'm with someone now."

"Who?"

"Billy Dixon."

Isabel pulled out her notepad and jotted down the name. "And his address?"

She cleared her throat. "He lives with me but he has a trailer that he lets out to a friend of mine. Her name's Carla."

"Who's she?"

"She used to work at the same hotel as me until she got fired."

"For what?"

Theresa looked as if she was growing tired of the questions. "Drug use."

"So what did Jack want?"

"He just wanted to see how I was."

"Did he give you the address of the hotel he was staying at?"

She didn't reply.

"Theresa. I'm trying to help here."

"What, by putting him away?"

"He's killed people. We can't just let him walk away. He has to be brought in and account for what he's done."

She reached across to her bedside table and grabbed a glass of water. She gulped it down and then placed it back.

"My daughter's name is Ruby."

"Did he go see her?"

"Yes."

Finally, she was making some progress. "What's your home address?"

Theresa blew out her cheeks. She gave it and as Isabel

was scribbling it down, she heard a commotion outside. At first she just thought it was an unruly mental health patient. It was common to see security being called in to assist with someone who was getting abusive to the nurses. But then she heard a scream. Isabel rose up from her seat and strode over to the door. She cracked it just a little to see what was going on.

* * *

Stupid security guards never learn. Giovanni had entered the hospital and made it up to the third floor without anyone seeing the Remington 870 Express Magnum that was under his jacket. It hung from a holster strap. Eighteen inches fit nicely beneath the jacket with just the tip of the barrel showing. He had managed to get the front desk to tell him the room number. When the security guard noticed the barrel and drew his weapon, he could have pulled it but instead Giovanni just palmed him in the face three times and tossed him down the stairwell.

It was only when a nurse saw him do it that the

screams started. Of course someone had to be a hero. He gave a warning but the guy didn't listen. Giovanni spun the shotgun up from underneath his jacket and fired a round into the guy who could have been an American football player by the sheer size of him. He flew back on to a gurney and landed in a heap, bleeding out. Panic ensued as people began running for cover.

* * *

"Shit!" Isabel pulled her weapon and looked back at Theresa. "Get out of bed now."

"What?"

Isabel hadn't taken her eyes off the man who was coming up the corridor. He forged forward with a confidence that she could tell came from years of experience. Another security guard came into view with his weapon drawn. He gave the assailant a warning but the approaching stranger didn't listen, he fired several rounds towards the security guard, sending paper and medical devices all over the place. The security guard returned fire, taking cover behind a desk.

Isabel moved over to Theresa, grabbed her by the arm and helped her out of bed. Barely able to walk, she groaned in pain as Isabel wrapped an arm around her shoulders and took most of her weight. At the door she glanced out one more time. The security guard was holding him back with multiple shots. She opened the door and glanced down the other end of the corridor. There was an exit stairwell.

"Are you ready?"

Theresa nodded and Isabel moved out. Bullets were ricocheting off the walls, large chunks of drywall flew in the air making the place look like it was snowing. Like a horse with blinders on, she focused on the door and practically dragged Theresa towards it. Each step of the way she could hear her wincing in pain. She had no idea if the people who were responsible for hurting Theresa had come to finish off the job, or if this was related to Jack. Either way she wasn't going to let the only person who could help her potentially catch Jack die.

With one arm wrapped around Theresa and the other

gripping her gun, she fired off several rounds and then shouldered the door to the stairway.

"Can you make it down?" she yelled.

She didn't need to ask her twice. Theresa held on to the handrail and started down the steep steps. Meanwhile Isabel pushed the door open and assisted the security guard who had now been hit in the arm. This guy was insane; he continued to press forward with little concern for whether he would be hit. Bullets peppered the wall close to her and she felt a chunk of concrete hit her in the face. She looked back at Theresa who had only made it down one flight of steps. There were two more to go. At this rate she wouldn't make it. Isabel pulled the fire alarm on the wall, abandoned her post and rushed down the stairs to help. The sound of police sirens could be heard echoing outside. As they continued down the next flight, Isabel kept looking up expecting the man to come bursting through the doors and fire at them, but he never appeared.

By the time they had made it down to the next floor,

the fire sprinkler system above had kicked in and water gushed out, turning the tiled floor into a slip and slide. Soaked, out of breath, and frantic to get her to safety, Isabel made a decision to head into the second floor level and get Theresa into a safe room while she reassessed the situation.

Isabel crouched in the doorway of a room, her eyes flitting up and down the corridor. Water streamed down her face as her eyes darted back and forth.

Seconds, then minutes passed. When she finally saw police enter she breathed a sigh of relief. She would later find out that the assailant had killed two security guards and escaped.

Chapter 18

When Jack received the phone call he was on his way to the hospital. He didn't recognize the number and for a moment he considered not answering it. With Agent Baker after him, he didn't know who she had been in contact with. Had she spoken to Theresa? She wasn't picking up so he'd decided to visit her at the hospital.

"Jack. It's me. Billy."

"Billy?"

"You said you wanted to help."

Jack snorted. He knew it wouldn't be long before Billy would call him.

"Go ahead."

"I think I know how to turn this situation around but I need your help carrying out a few things."

"What is it?"

"Probably best I show you. Can you meet me in ten minutes at a coffee house on Columbia Street?"

Jack ran a hand through his hair. "I was on my way to the hospital."

"We have less than twenty-four hours."

Jack sighed. "I can be there in an hour."

He didn't like the guy and he definitely didn't like the fact that he wouldn't tell him what he needed help with, but if it meant making sure they were safe, it was worth it.

* * *

Jack placed a phone call to Jamaar and he was more than happy to take him. It would be roughly a fifty-minute drive. Along the way Jamaar kept on asking him questions about what he did for a living. It was then that he'd remembered that he'd forgotten to get back in touch with the woman who had phoned him for help. Shit! He berated himself. Whatever hope he had of carving out a living helping others was going to have to wait. Since getting out of prison he had spent more time helping others for free. Had it not been for the money that Eddie had left behind he would have been begging on the streets by now.

"So what business are you in?"

Sitting in the back of the cab he barely heard what Jamaar had asked him over the noise of the music that was blaring out of his speakers. He had in his hand the scrap of paper with Dana's new address and number. He had considered phoning her but after all the shit that he'd been through, there was no way in hell he was going to drag her back into it. Though he was curious to know how she and Jason were doing. Had the agent badgered them for details about where he was and what he had done? Had Dana told her?

"I do a bit of this, and that."

Jamaar laughed. "I hear you, mon, you have to have your hand in a lot of jars nowadays just to pay your way."

"How long have you been driving?"

"Good question." He lowered the volume on the radio. Perhaps he shouldn't have asked him that. He was the kind of guy who made his business from talking to clients. All cabbies were either super silent or you couldn't get them to shut up. There was no happy medium.

"It's got to be coming up eleven years. I did it for a while back in my home country but there wasn't hardly any money to be made in it. Besides, I had my fair share of criminals rob me. That's why I got the hell out of there. What about you? Where do you come from?"

"New York."

"You are far from home."

"It's not home."

He had no idea where home was. New York had been all he had ever known. For a short while Rockland Cove was home but that was just a vague memory now.

"What about family? You have a lady that keeps you warm at night? Kids?"

Had anyone asked him that a few months ago he would have laughed. Jack pocketed the number and pulled out the photo of Ruby. He handed it to Jamaar. Jamaar looked down then back at the road in front of him.

"Cute kid. She's yours?"

"Yeah. Well, I think so."

"Oh. Baby momma wasn't honest with yah?"

"I'm not sure," he replied taking the photo back from him. "What about you?"

"No mon, I love the single life too much. I tried it for a while. You know the whole trying to settle down but…" He blew out a puff of smoke. "They want to change you. You know. Like she was sweet and all but then when she moved in, she got all crazy like. Telling me where to put my clothes, and what I should do. I felt like she was suffocating me. It didn't last. That's when I moved here."

"And kids?"

He flipped the visor down above him. Attached to the visor with a clip was a photo of two boys. One looked around ten years of age, the other around seven. He tapped the photo and a big smile spread across his face.

"My boys."

"You don't miss them?"

"Every day but down in Jamaica I couldn't offer them anything. I could barely rub together two dollars."

"Will you return?"

"No, if I can get enough money I will bring them up here. It's a better life than there."

When Jack arrived at the café, he handed Jamaar some green and told him to wait while he looked around for Billy. He had no idea if he would show up or if he was just messing him around. When he spotted him inside drinking from a cup, he leaned down into the window and told Jamaar that if he wanted to hang around he probably would catch a ride back with him. He told him he would give him enough to cover for the day. He just wanted to make sure he had a ride back to the French Quarter.

Jamaar agreed and told him he would park his cab over in the lot across the street. "Any problem, just call me."

Jack nodded and entered the café. Billy was tapping his fingers against his leg. His eyes darted around the room as Jack came over.

"I thought you weren't going to show."

"It's a long ride. This better be worth it."

"It is. Twenty minutes of your time and I'll have this

all dealt with. No one will get harmed. Come on, my ride is out front."

"Where's Ruby?"

"Carla is looking after her."

That meant no one was looking after her. Jack ground his teeth.

Jack joined him in a beat-up Chevy truck and they rolled out. Inside it was disgusting. Coffee cups all over the floor, and a sweatshirt on the ground that stank of beer and oil. The seats themselves were cracked. Foam was sticking out and he could even feel the springs beneath him. Across the front of his window were old parking tickets and dead flies. In the middle console the ashtray was full of blunts.

"So what is this all about?"

"You'll see."

The truck bumped its way around the town and out towards the outskirts. Billy took a left turn down a dirt road that led up to a large house that he imagined was owned by a farmer as all around the land looked as if it had been tilled and prepared for crops to be grown. A large brown fence ran around the perimeter. As they came up to the clapboard house, Billy pulled up in front and hopped out. Jack followed him up to the door and then Billy paused.

"I didn't leave the door open."

He pulled out a gun that he had tucked under his shirt behind him and that immediately placed Jack on alert. Jack reached for his as they ventured in. Inside it was dark. No curtains had been opened. Billy pressed forward towards the back room as if he knew where he was going. As he disappeared around a corner he let out a high-pitched cry. Jack readied himself for a confrontation but it never happened. Joining him, he observed Billy frantically looking around the ground, then inside a room. He banged his fist against the side of his head.

"Shit," he cried and proceeded to kick over a table and smash a lamp.

"What's going on?" Jack said keeping his gun lowered.

"It was right here. I left it right here."

"What?"

"The meth. Packets of it. There had to have been at least a hundred grand in meth."

"Whose house is this?"

"A friend of mine."

"And where's he?"

"In there. Dead."

Jack didn't believe him at first. He headed into the room that Billy was in and peered around the corner. Sure enough, there was a body lying on the ground with a bullet wound in the back of the head.

"Did you do this?"

He nodded. Still holding the gun in his hand he scratched his head and slumped down on the leather sofa before kicking his legs up onto the table.

"I'm so dead."

Jack stared at the dead man and the empty room.

"Go back to the beginning. What happened?"

Billy began moaning as if he was in pain, then he started smashing his own fist into the side of his head.

"Stupid. Stupid. Stupid."

Jack was starting to get a little bit pissed off by this guy. Billy brought him up to speed on what he had done that morning and everything that he had in mind.

"So you were just going to rob him?"

"No. He owed me money and I knew he was dealing. I just thought he could give me the forty grand but I should have guessed he wouldn't. If I didn't put a bullet in him, he would have done it to me."

"Are you sure about that?"

"Who cares? It doesn't matter now."

"Well, who do you think took it?"

"How the hell should I know? His partners? Whoever else was staying here."

Chapter 19

Isabel got off the phone with Simon after giving him an update. He wasn't in the best mood so she never told him about the incident in the hotel but the hospital shooting had been all over the news. She tried to reassure him that it was under control. He didn't believe her. She was getting closer but he didn't see it that way. It was all excuses.

"Find him or I will put someone else on this and you'll be filling out reports for the department until you retire."

"You have my word."

Her word was shot. She was in way over her head and she knew it. This wasn't just about hunting down Jack Winchester, she was now being pulled into whatever shit Theresa had got herself caught up in.

After she had been seen to by medics, the hospital placed Theresa in a different ward and the security was doubled on the hospital. Soaked from the sprinklers,

Isabel badly wanted to get out of her clothes, take a hot shower and slip into something less sticky but that was going to have to wait.

"You are not telling me something, Theresa. Now what is it?"

She looked embarrassed, scared and Isabel could tell she had her where she wanted her. It was one thing to be threatened by the FBI, and another to find yourself running for your life.

"These men aren't going to stop, Theresa. I can't help you, if you don't tell me what happened. The hospital says you were raped and beaten. But by who?"

"I don't know. I told you that. I didn't know the men. Billy got himself caught up in something and now he owes them money."

Isabel nodded, now it was starting to make sense.

"And how's Jack fit into all of this? Does Billy owe him money?"

"No. I told you he's not involved in any of this."

"Where can I find Billy?"

Theresa's chin dropped. "Come on, Theresa, we are going around in circles here."

"He phoned earlier. Before you came. Said he needed Jack's number."

"You have Jack's number?"

She had let the cat out of the bag. A look spread across her face, the realization that she had just dropped the ball.

"Give me the number, Theresa."

"My phone is in my bag. You are going to arrest him, aren't you?"

"I'm going to talk to him."

She hadn't really thought about what she was going to do. She had the New Orleans police at her disposal and she could phone in for backup from U.S. Marshals, but now she wasn't dealing with one killer, she had two. Who was the other one? Maybe she could catch two birds with one stone. It certainly would appease Simon and his superiors. The question was, who was the man who came into the hospital working for? Was he part of the group that had beaten Theresa? Or was he Mafia-related?

After she retrieved her cell phone she took down the number and then handed the phone to Theresa.

"Call him."

"What do you want me to say?"

"Tell him exactly what happened except you're not going to mention me."

"But he'll show up here."

"Exactly."

Chapter 20

Jack paced back and forth. On one hand he wanted to smack Billy around and knock some sense into him and on the other he realized that time was ticking. When his phone started ringing, he glanced at Billy who was entertaining a pity party of one with a bottle of beer. Jack stepped into the kitchen. It was Theresa.

"You okay?"

"Yeah. There's been a bit of an incident down here."

"What happened?"

"You near a TV?"

"Yeah, hold on."

Jack snagged up the clicker and switched it on. He switched it to the channel she gave and turned up the volume. Video showed the outside of the hospital and a reporter. Lots of police and medics were in the background. Fire trucks had their lights flashing.

From what we have managed to learn today, there was only one person involved. The assailant was in his late thirties. So far there have been two casualties. They will be releasing the names of the victims but it's believed they were security guards. There's been no mention of anyone else injured. But people today are shaken up here in New Orleans. Now we have a witness here who says she saw the man.

A woman in scrubs came into the frame.

I was just getting ready to finish my shift when I heard the gunshots. I was at the front desk and I spoke to the man. He wanted directions to a room of a patient.

The reporter pressed her for more details.

What did he look like? Can you describe what he said?

The woman looked as if she was about to speak when a police officer came over and cut the interview short. Jack looked on in shock.

"Are you sure you're okay?"

"He was coming for me, Jack."

"How do you know that?"

Before she answered him, she blurted out, "Jack, the FBI is here."

The moment she said that, Jack heard a scuffle as if Theresa was wrestling for control of the phone. Suddenly it stopped and he heard her voice for the first time.

"Jack Winchester. I'm Agent Baker —"

Jack cut her off. "I know who you are."

"Then you know that I have to bring you in."

"I'm not coming in. I've done my time."

"Not for the killings in L.A."

Jack didn't reply. The FBI was known for recording conversation and then using it later in court as admissible evidence. Jack glanced back into the living room where Billy was. He squeezed the bridge of his nose feeling the weight of the world closing in on him.

"Who shot up that hospital?"

Now it was Isabel's turn to go quiet.

"I thought you might know. Is Billy there?"

"What are you going to do with Theresa?"

"That depends on you, Jack. I don't want to charge

her but I will."

"She has a daughter."

Isabel chuckled on the other end of the line. "Yeah, I heard you are a father now. Do you want your kid to grow up knowing that you killed people?"

"You don't understand."

"No. I understand. I've learned a lot about you over the past few months, Jack, and I have got to say that you are a danger to society."

"Perhaps."

"Why don't you just make this easy for everyone and come on in?"

"Like I said, I can't do that."

Jack hung up on her before she could say any more. He pocketed the phone and went back into the living room. He grabbed Billy by the arm and yanked him up.

"Man, what the hell?" Billy protested.

"You're going to take me to Tex."

"I told you I don't know where he is. When they took me in I had a bag over my head. You don't get to see him.

He brings you to him."

"Think! Who is responsible for taking these drugs?"

"I…"

"Don't say you don't know or I will shoot you here where you stand."

He looked as if he was trying to think. "Well, I mean. He said he had a new guy that was cooking up batches of meth for him. But before that, he worked with a guy by the name of Markus. He might know. He might even still work for him."

"Right, let's head on over to his place."

"I need to phone him and find out the address."

He stared back blankly. "Well, go on then."

Billy went back through the kitchen and into the living room area where he had first sat down with Mike. He looked on the table but his phone was gone. Frantically he searched around on the floor and under the chairs before he kicked the table. That was followed by a fit of rage and he proceeded to smash anything and everything that was within reach. When he was done he was panting hard and sweating. He cursed and picked up a bottle of beer and chugged it back.

"I'm guessing by your horrid attempt at redecorating this place that you've got more bad news?"

"My phone is gone."

Right then, Jack's phone rang. He looked down and saw the caller ID was Theresa. The agent was trying to get back through to him again. He declined the call. She wasn't going to give up. Things were spiraling out of control real fast. He'd wasted enough time with this bonehead. If he hadn't got involved with drugs, they wouldn't be in this position.

He took out his gun and pressed it against Billy's head.

"I'm all out of patience. You better know who we need to go see right now or I'm going to put a bullet through your thick skull."

He threw his hands up all defensive like. "Okay. Okay. I know someone who might know."

Chapter 21

Frustrated at the way the conversation had gone, Isabel still had no idea where he was. Theresa had practically shut down. The only lead she had was an address for Billy and Theresa's home address. She arranged for a police officer to remain outside her hospital room before she left for Covington.

There was no point attempting to get a trace on Jack's phone, he would have tossed it by now. All along the way she thought about what she would say when she saw him next. What should have been a simple matter of negotiating with him had gone south real quick. She was going to play the daughter card but he'd hung up before she could use it as a means to lure him back. All phone calls to him after went unanswered.

She had called ahead to Covington police to have them meet her at the trailer park. This had been the first case where she didn't feel safe. No matter how she reasoned things out in her mind, Jack was still a killer, even if he hadn't shot at her. It's not like she hadn't considered what Detective Banfield or Theresa had said about Jack's character. She'd seen many a person turn around from a lifestyle of criminal behavior but that didn't give him a free pass. He still had to be held accountable.

As the GPS in her rental gave her the final turn, she pulled into the trailer park and found two cruisers waiting for her. The cops were talking with the owner of the park by the looks of it. He was pointing in a direction. When they saw her get out and flash her badge, they asked how they could help. She hadn't asked them to go into the trailer. She wanted to be there in the event that Billy was inside.

The wind had picked up, and a light rain was coming down.

"I've never had a problem with him. He's always paid on time. He has someone else staying there at the moment. Carla. No complaints from neighbors. I have to say this is a first for us," the owner said. He was a tubby, partially bald man with hair that shot out the sides of his head like a clown. He was wearing a clean shirt, pants and polished shoes. For someone who owned a trailer park, he looked very professional. Though, what remained of his hair could have used some work.

Isabel showed the owner Jack's mug shot and his eyes immediately lit up.

"Yeah. Yeah. He was here. I saw him with Carla for a while and then Billy's daughter."

"Where did he head off to?"

"I think he took her home. I'm not sure."

Isabel approached the door, knocked a few times and stood off to one side. She had experienced her fair share of crazies who shot through the door at the first sign of police showing up. It didn't matter if they were wanted or not. The general public freaked out at the sign of red and blue flashing lights.

There was no answer. She tried again. The other officers had their weapons drawn and were focusing on the windows. Isabel reached over and turned the knob on the door. It opened and she pulled it wide. A few seconds passed. She called out Jack's name first. No answer. She followed up by asking for Carla or Billy. Still no reply. Cautiously she stepped up inside the trailer. Her heart was fluttering in her chest as she fully expected to be shot at. Instead she was met by an aroma of death.

Moving quickly through the trailer she made her way to the bedroom. Lying on the bed with a bullet in the head was a young woman. She couldn't have been more than twenty-five years of age. She was partially dressed. On the side table was drug paraphernalia. Isabel called out to the one of the officers to bring in the owner of the trailer park.

A few seconds passed before he joined her inside. The moment he saw her he nearly threw up. "Oh god, that's her. That's Carla." The officer led him out and Isabel came outside. Had Jack killed her?

"Tape it off and don't let anyone inside," she said. She took two officers with her to Theresa's home. It was a short distance by car and they were there within five minutes. On the outside everything looked normal. No sign of entry. Her first concern was for the safety of the child. Theresa had said that her daughter was with Carla. There was no sign of her except a pink Hello Kitty bag laying on the floor inside the trailer.

One of the officers went around the back while the other one approached the main entrance. She repeated the same process of knocking and calling out for the resident to come out but there was no answer. Using the back of her weapon she broke the glass on the front door and reached inside to unlock it.

Glass crunched beneath her feet as she stepped in. It was dark inside. All the curtains had been drawn. Surprisingly the place was clean. It was clear to see that the home had a woman's touch. The officers went down the corridor one way, while she went into the living room. One by one they cleared the rooms. There was no one there. She called out for Ruby, in the chance that she had hidden, but no sound was heard.

Outside she visited the neighbor's homes to check if

Ruby was staying with anyone else. No one had seen her and they hadn't seen Billy since that morning.

That's when she had the police run an Amber Alert. She wasn't going to chase them all over Louisiana, and she didn't give two hoots about what her boss had to say. She made sure it included details about Ruby being accompanied by Billy Dixon or Jack Winchester. Their mug shots would be shown beside hers. Beneath their faces it would say PERSON OF INTEREST.

Chapter 22

Twenty minutes away on the other side of the town, Jack burst through a door of an apartment block that Billy said belonged to a dealer that went by the name Leafy. Billy had made it clear that he didn't open his door to anyone except those he trusted. Billy wasn't one of them.

"How many will there be inside?"

"Three, maybe four tops. But I'm telling yah, these guys don't fuck around. One of them will phone Tex's men while the others are putting lead in you."

As the door slammed against the wall, the first guy who came into view was wearing nothing more than a pair of boxer shorts and a string vest. His eyes lit up with pure panic as Jack charged in with his Glock aimed at his head. He threw his hands up and backed up against the wall. Jack grabbed him by the neck and shoved him into the living room. The place was in a filthy state; beer bottles, cigarettes and bags of meth all over the table. One black dude was lying down with a naked girl on top of him when they came into the room. Jack's eyes darted around the room assessing the situation. One on the couch and another sprawled out with a needle in his arm. The door to the bedroom opened up. He didn't have a choice, the guy had a shotgun in hand. Jack tried to give him a warning but he was wired, jacked up on meth or some shit as he raised the shotgun up. Jack tossed the scrawny fella in front of him and he received the full force of the shot giving Jack enough time to fire a round into the shooter. Meanwhile Billy was wheeling his gun around the room at the two other men.

"That's my shit."

Billy picked up a bag and looked it over.

"Where did you get this?"

A large guy who probably was meant to be the muscle of the group but was as slow as a snail replied. "Ronny dropped it off. He told us there was more where that came from and if we wanted to buy, they were now in the market."

"Ronny?"

"Who is he?" Jack asked.

"He's a new cook in town."

"Was."

The guy eyed his other pal nervously.

"Did he give you an address, a number?" Jack asked.

The fat guy with his hands still up pointed to his phone on the table. "I have his digits in there."

Billy motioned to him to phone him. "You even give him the slightest inclination that there is trouble, I will redecorate this room with your insides. You understand?"

Jack wasn't impressed by Billy's macho shit but as long as it got them what they needed and put an end to this, that's all he was bothered about.

"What about Tex?"

The guy had his hand on the phone. "I don't have his number."

"Bullshit," Billy said. "One of you does."

The black guy pointed to the one who was writhing

around on the floor with a bullet in his leg. "Tommy has it. But he won't give it up. Tex will kill us if he finds out."

Jack went over to the guy who tried to shuffle back. Jack tried the straightforward approach. "You wanna tell us where he is?"

"Fuck you."

He tried going for the shotgun again, so Jack kicked him in the face.

"Let's try that again."

"I'm not giving you assholes anything."

Jack looked back at Billy briefly before stepping on the guy's injured leg. The guy screamed in pain for a minute until Jack released the pressure. "Now I don't have all day."

"He will kill me if I give it out."

Jack stepped on his leg again, crouched down and took a hold of the guy's ear, giving it a little twist in the process. "No, he won't as you'll already be dead."

The guy's pupils were dilated. He was as high as a kite.

He looked as if he had been up several days. Meth did that. It would make them feel invincible until they crashed. Most addicts would go on benders for days, commit most of their crimes in that time and then spend the next day or two shaking until they got their next hit. It was a wicked cycle that never let up until it spat you out.

"Okay, I'll get it for you."

The scrawny little punk got up and dragged his bleeding leg across the room to a set of drawers. He pulled the top one out and started tossing a whole bunch of papers all over the floor. He then went into the next drawer and did the same, however this time he pulled a gun. Jack reacted before he had a chance to fire it. One bullet in the head and it was over.

"You idiot!" Billy said, rushing over and bouncing up and down a bit.

"He didn't have it."

"How do you know?"

"Trust me. In my line of work, you can tell when

someone is just trying to buy themselves some time."

They were about to turn their attention back to the other guys when they noticed the black guy had made a dash for it. The large guy, knowing he wasn't getting out of this alive, chose a different route. The other one had got up and was close to the window when Billy turned the gun on him.

"Don't even think about it," he said.

"Where do you meet Tex?"

"Fuck you. I'm not telling you anything."

Jack went over and gave him a few slaps around the head.

"You think for one minute that any one of us are going to sign our own death warrant?"

Jack had to admit; he'd seen mob bosses use intimidation to keep men loyal. Fear was a good motivator. Gafino had it down to a fine art. Rarely ever would someone think of squealing on him. It wasn't death they feared. It was what would happen before death gave them peace. No doubt Tex had made quite the

JON MILLS

impression on these guys. If Billy's story about the alligator was true, then what came next was to be expected.

"You are going…"

Before Billy could finish what he was saying, the fat guy launched himself through a closed window. They were ten stories up. After the sound of glass shattering came the thud of a body hitting the roof of a car and setting off a car alarm that startled them. Billy raced to the window and looked out before slipping back inside. "Holy shit."

As surprising as it was to Billy, Jack had seen it many times before. Those he'd been sent to collect on sometimes chose to fall to their death rather than face the unexpected. They knew they would die, but this way they determined how they went.

"Get his phone, let's go find Ronny."

"The guy just launched himself out the window," Billy stammered.

"Even more reason to hurry."

198

Billy raised both hands and shrugged as if he couldn't wrap his head around it. Jack wasn't in the mood for anyone slowing him down. He went over and grabbed him by the back of the neck.

"If you don't pull shit together, you are going out the window."

Billy swallowed hard and scooped up the phone on the table. He flipped through it until he found Ronny's number. They could hear sirens in the distance.

"Just take it with you. We've got to get out of here."

Chapter 23

Charley "Tex" Wilson was sitting in the back yard of his home watching his kid celebrate his sixth birthday. Beside him were two hulking men that he employed for protection. He never went anywhere without them. For over twenty years he had worked his way to establish himself as the main distributor for meth in Louisiana. Unlike those he once worked for, he wasn't afraid to get his hands covered in blood. It's what kept his men loyal. He let them see his murderous acts. He made a spectacle out of those who challenged his authority. It was the only way to keep those around him in line.

The meth business was booming even though the DEA and local police were constantly breathing down his neck, raiding his labs and hauling away mammoth amounts of money. It came with the territory.

He didn't want to remain in the business for long. With every year that passed, new gangs were trying to move in and take a piece of what was his. He looked over at Kalen, his eldest. Twenty-four and still learning the ropes, Tex had done everything within his power to ensure that his son could carry on the business after he pulled out, but now he was starting to think that it was too risky even for his own flesh and blood.

Francis, his bodyguard, came over and whispered in his ear that he had a phone call. He thanked him and took a few seconds to excuse himself from the party. His wife, Gillian, looked at him to once again show her disgust. She was a good woman and was one of the many reasons why he wanted to get out of the business. He'd been with her since he was seventeen. She had seen his rise and seen him come close to losing everything. If it hadn't been for her constant badgering, he might not have considered a future beyond selling drugs.

Back when he was young, everything had been low-key. He was one of many distributors, much like Billy. He had done his time dealing on the streets, been through the period of hiring others to do his dirty work until he saw the opportunity to branch out on his own. Back then as long as a person wasn't doing over a hundred grand a month, those he worked for didn't bat an eye. They were too busy making money.

Once Tex took the place of the guy who had originally hired him as a distributor, things moved quickly. He soon found the quickest way to earn more money without the risk was not to bring in more drugs. It was to manage the drug dealers who were already selling meth. The homegrown operations that barely brought in twenty grand a week were usually run by some punk who thought he could make a fast buck using the simple shake and bake method of producing meth. It worked. Except they weren't accountable to anyone until Tex came along. That's what made him different from his previous bosses. He wasn't interested in making large deals which could turn bad fast. No, it was much easier to bang on the doors of known small-time dealers and get them paying him seventy-five percent of all of their business. Within a matter of two years he brought in more than his bosses had in five years in business. He also didn't have to deal with the cops busting him. They were the ones at risk, not him.

It was a win-win situation. He supplied local dealers with pseudoephedrine, which meant they didn't have to go into drugstores. In return they gave him the largest percentage of profits. There wasn't one dealer who couldn't see this as a good thing. Up until that point the cops were nabbing small-time meth dealers by catching them after they left drugstores. Now they didn't need to go into stores. They just came to him. He'd worked out a lucrative deal with the Mexicans to bring in large amounts of pseudoephedrine using the same connections that his previous bosses had used.

Tex took the phone and stepped out of the sunshine. He stood at the window watching his child play. A constant reminder to him about what life was really about.

"Hello?"

"Tex. It's Matt Randall."

"Matt. How are things going with production?"

"Yeah, about that. Mike is dead."

"What?"

Tex walked away from the window. He squinted trying to comprehend what this would mean to his bottom line.

"The product? Have you retrieved it?"

"It's gone."

"What do you mean it's gone?"

"The boys and I went around there earlier today. The place had been cleaned out. That's when we found Mike. He'd been shot in the back of the head."

"Who did this?"

"We're not sure but we found a cell phone on the table. Get this. It belongs to Billy Dixon."

Tex nodded his head and gritted his teeth. It was beginning to make sense.

"What do you want us to do?"

"Besides bringing me his fucking head?" Tex paused to breathe in deeply. He was seething with anger. Even though Mike wasn't aware that Tex was his supplier, Mike had become one of his best dealers. It wasn't like he couldn't cook up more batches but out of all the dealers he worked with, Mike had distributed a large percentage. Whoever took the meth would pay for this. "Keep your eye out for him."

"Will do."

"And Matt. Thanks."

"Sure thing, Tex."

He hung up and stood there squeezing the phone tightly. He tossed it across the room and it shattered on the wall just as Kalen came in.

"Whoa, Pops. What's going on?"

"Billy Dixon."

He brought him up to speed on what had taken place.

"I told you, you should have killed him."

Tex eyed his son with contempt. He didn't like having anyone tell him what do, especially if they were right. He inwardly cursed his decision to give him more time. In all the times he'd ever been lenient with people, they had double-crossed him or tried to run. Kalen was learning fast. Tex knew business would continue to flourish in his hands. Perhaps it was time to step down and let his son take the reins. He walked back to the window and looked at his six-year-old playing.

"Find him. Bring him to me."

"But doesn't he have until the end of the day?"

"No. His time's up. And get his bitch and daughter too."

With that he ventured back outside with a smile on his face as though nothing had unsettled him. It was all about keeping his family happy.

Chapter 24

He had contemplated shooting her but when the woman told him that it was Jack's daughter he thought he had hit the jackpot. He was growing tired of chasing him. The incident at the hospital had been unavoidable but it meant the police might discover what he looked like. He had no time to find the security cameras. Right now he needed to stay off the streets at least until it got dark in a few hours. Giovanni had holed up in a seedy motel on the outskirts of Covington called the Sunrise Motel.

The room was cramped, dirty and still stuck in the sixties by the looks of the place. He had pushed a twenty-five cent piece into the machine beside the bed and it started vibrating. Since arriving the kid hadn't moved from the corner. Crouched down with her arms wrapped around her knees, she cowered every time he got close. He had no qualms about killing her. He'd done it before. He didn't like it but if it came down to him being taken in by the police he would do whatever was necessary.

He pointed to the bed hoping to keep her occupied with its shaking. But she just looked away. He flicked the TV on and put it on some kids channel but she ignored it.

"You hungry?"

There was no response. She wasn't mute as she was wailing up a storm after he had killed that bitch back in the trailer. Now that was one crazy tweaker. She had tried to stab him. Had she played it cool and told him where Jack was, maybe he wouldn't have beaten her to a pulp.

"What about a drink? You like Coke?"

She nodded. He scanned the room looking for something to tie her to while he stepped out. He went over to her and grabbed her by the arm. She started crying as he brought her into the bathroom. He pulled his belt off and she must have thought she was going to get a licking. Instead he used it to bind her wrists and then attach her to the towel rack.

"Stay still. Be quiet. I will be back soon."

He stepped out and looked back at her. She didn't look like a runner. Tears streaked her face and for a brief moment he thought of his own daughter. The memory stung. He left the room and wandered down to a vending machine he'd seen near the registration office. As he pushed a dollar into the machine he looked through the window and saw the guy in the office looking up at the TV. A picture of the girl's face, along with Jack Winchester and someone else, came on the screen. The cops were looking for her. He pushed a button and the can clunked as it fell down into the slot at the bottom. He took it out. It was warm. What the hell? Giovanni went over to the office and stuck his head inside.

"Your soda machine isn't working. Damn thing is warm."

"Been like that for months," the guy replied.

He sighed and returned to the room. When he came inside he glanced towards the bathroom but she was gone. He dropped the can and his eyes darted around the room. He heard her before he saw her. The little brat had managed to get out of her binds and had hidden. He turned to grab her but she was like a little jackrabbit. She shot out the door yelling. He bolted out after her. She was running across the gravel in bare feet. She hadn't made it twenty feet when he scooped her up and tossed her over his shoulder.

"Shut the hell up."

"Let me go."

He muffled her cries with his hand and brought her back into the room. As he was stepping inside, he saw the man in the office glance out. *Shit!*

He didn't have time to bind her. He tossed her inside the room and locked the door behind her. He heard her banging on the door as he moved towards the office. As he walked inside, the guy was already on the phone. Giovanni held a gun up and the guy slowly placed the phone down. He gestured for him to go into the back.

"Take a seat."

The guy was in his late fifties. He sat down with his hands up. Terror was written across his face.

"You the only one who works here?"

"No. There are a few of us that take shifts. This is mine. I'm here until ten."

"I really wish you hadn't made that phone call."

"I didn't even get through to them. I promise, I won't say anything."

Giovanni reached into his pocket, took out a suppressor and proceeded to screw it on the end.

"Please. I won't tell."

"You promise?" he asked sarcastically. It was always the same with those who were about to die. They would tell you anything. Anything to get out of their situation. If you let them go, the same people would face you in court saying how strong they were. It was all bullshit. They weren't strong. If anyone got away, it was because of luck.

"Yeah." The guy nodded with a look of hope in his eyes. That quickly changed when Giovanni leveled the gun at his head and a bullet lodged itself in his skull. Blood hit the back of the wall and brain matter dripped down. Killing was a lot like anything else. At first he was horrified at the sight of blood. He felt an immense amount of guilt. That soon subsided and pulling the trigger was as easy as breathing. No remorse. No guilt. Nothing prevented him from sleeping at night. He had no preference on who died. It all came down to risk. He left no one behind alive. He sat there thinking of what it would be like to put a bullet in Jack Winchester. He felt nothing for the man. It wasn't like he had done him any harm. Giovanni's connection to him was purely motivated by a desire to repay Salvatore for what he had done for his mother. He didn't care about Salvatore. He didn't see him as a father, even though he was his biological one. This was all business. A means to an end. Once it was completed he wouldn't have to think that his mother owed anything.

Giovanni took a few seconds to breathe in deeply before he placed the gun back inside his jacket and went to the main door to check if anyone was looking. In frustration he slammed his fist against the side of the drywall leaving a large dent. Outside there was a large ice box. For a moment he considered placing him in it but then decided otherwise. For all he knew the guy had got through to the police and alerted them to the girl.

He closed the door behind him and returned to the room.

"Get your stuff."

"Are you taking me home?"

"Just do as you're told."

The kid rushed over to the corner where she had laid her jacket. He took a firm grip on her hand and led her out to his car. He put her in the back and secured her in. He didn't wait or linger a second longer. He drove out of there and into Goodbee, one town over. There he found another motel and paid for the night. He wasn't going to risk the chance of police showing up at the different motels in Covington. Once he got the key he unlocked the door to his room and grabbed up the girl. This time he was careful not to take her out of the car until he was sure that no one was looking. He returned to the car and from the back he pulled out some old zip ties from his bag. He secured her wrists to the foot of the bed, shut the curtains and tried to settle in for the night. Nothing about what he was doing felt rushed. He had all the time in the world to finish the job. Right now he was holding the winning lottery ticket. If Jack didn't know already about his little girl, by tomorrow he would. Either way, Jack wasn't going anywhere.

Giovanni turned on the TV and flipped through until he saw warnings about the hurricane. He snorted. Hurricane? He hadn't felt anything but some light rain and wind. Then the camera flipped to shots of Lake Pontchartrain, Lake Borgne and other areas that viewers had taken video of. Waves were wild and what looked like a terrible storm was beginning to brew on the horizon.

"What's your name, kid?"

She hesitated before she replied. "Ruby."

On the screen came another Amber warning. "Do you recognize this other man?"

"Jack is a friend of my mother's."

Giovanni frowned then clued in. "The other one is

your father?"

She nodded. Why had Carla said that Jack Winchester was her father? Unless of course Theresa had got knocked up before arriving in Louisiana.

"How old are you, kid?"

"Eight."

"And how long have you been living here?"

"For as long as I remember."

He stared at her and thought of his own daughter. Would Jack hand himself over if he knew his daughter's life was hanging in the balance? He thought back to the men who had taken his wife and daughter. The pain of the past ached in his heart. He saw their faces before him. He heard their tears and listened to the demands of the men he eventually killed.

The memories were too painful. Outside the wind picked up and lightning flashed. A sudden crack of thunder and he was no longer thinking about all that he'd lost.

Chapter 25

It was late. A little after eleven at night when Billy made the phone call. They were initially going to return home but when they saw the cruiser lights in the distance, Billy took Jack to a bar on the west side called Murphy's Hole. There was hardly anyone inside. Just a couple of old guys sitting on bar stools shooting the breeze. One booth was taken by a young couple who looked like they were about to start having sex by the way they were groping each other.

Jack slid in across from Billy and ordered a double bourbon while Billy tried to get in contact with Ronny. He kept the phone on speakerphone.

"Ronny?"

"Yeah."

Billy glanced at Jack. "I heard you have some new product that's come in."

"Who is this?"

"It's Doug Jenkins. A friend of Mike's."

There was silence. Billy put his hand over the receiver and muttered something along the lines of this wasn't going to work. He was convinced that if Ronny was the one that had taken the drugs, he would be expecting a call.

"How much do you need?"

"How much you got?"

"Didn't Mike tell you?"

"No. He just said it was good and worth the money."

"Listen, you tell me how much you want and I'll tell you if I have enough."

"Forty grand."

"You distributing?"

"Here and there."

"That's a lot. I'll phone you back."

"No—"

The phone went dead and Billy sighed. "I told you it would spook him."

"He'll call back."

"The fuck he will. He's probably getting rid of it while we speak."

Jack shook his head. There was one thing you could count on with a dealer. Greed. It didn't matter how much risk was involved. They couldn't pass up a chance to make some nice green. Billy asked for the barman to bring over a beer. He lit a cigarette and Jack frowned.

"You know you can't smoke in here."

He took a portion of the packet from his cigarettes and tore the cardboard and used it as an ashtray. Faint jazz music played in the background. Jack saw the young couple get up and leave. Billy glanced at them before looking back at Jack.

"So how long have you known Theresa?" Billy asked.

Jack was taking a sip of his drink. He swallowed. "Since she was eighteen. And you? How did you meet her?"

He chuckled a little and tapped his cigarette. A chunk of ash broke off.

"I worked behind the desk at the hotel."

"You worked in a hotel?" Jack acted surprised.

"I was trying to do the right thing." He paused. "My mother, she's a religious woman. Has always been going on at me about leading a righteous life." He snorted. "Like what does that even mean?"

The barman came over and placed his beer on a coaster in front of him. "Thanks, Henry." He slipped him some cash and the barman walked away without even asking him to put out the cigarette.

"Anyway, she was working there. One thing led to another and we started seeing one another."

"How old was Ruby?"

"Three."

"So she's only ever known you."

He studied Jack, and squinted a little as smoke stung his eyes. "If you're wondering does she think I'm her father. Yeah. She does."

"And Theresa never told you who the real father is?"

He snorted. "Let's not beat around the bush here. I know she's yours."

"How long have you known that?"

"Since she told Carla. Yeah, I guess she still thinks I don't know. But I do."

"That doesn't bother you?"

He shrugged taking another hard pull on his cigarette. The end glowed a bright orange in the darkness before he exhaled.

"What about you? What do you do?"

"I haven't decided yet."

He frowned finding Jack's reply confusing. But it was true, Jack really hadn't given much thought to what he wanted to do with his life and now with the FBI on his ass any chance of him being able to hold down a regular job was pretty slim. He could have got out of town but it would have been no different than now. He'd always be looking over his shoulder. At least here he could try and make sure Theresa and Ruby were safe before he moved on.

"What did you do to end up inside?" Billy asked.

Jack downed the remainder of his drink and asked the

bartender for another.

"What makes you think that?"

"The look in your eye. Everyone inside gets it. It's a look of distrust. You know when I was inside, I was never afraid of what the other inmates would do to me. It was the guards I was worried about. Any one of them could have been paid a hundred bucks to kill me in my cell. I'm surprised Tex didn't do it that way."

"No, by the sounds of it, he likes to see those he kills squirm."

Billy nodded.

"You only did a year?" Jack asked.

"And the rest."

"How many times?"

"Twice. The last time I got out, well, you know before going back in, I was really trying to go straight. I moved back from Texas to here and started all over again, but you know how things are."

"No." Jack knew but he wanted to hear it from him.

"How am I supposed to give Theresa or Ruby a good

life on minimum wage? I was working forty hours a week for chump change," Billy said.

"That's called going straight."

He knew what was coming. He'd heard it countless times from buddies who did time inside and got out. They all justified why they had to return to crime. It was like they couldn't see their way to doing what everyone else did in the world. So strong was the pull of crime it would keep a person in a cycle of doing the same bad things. Since he'd got out, Jack had felt it. It was like an addiction. It wasn't the thrill of doing wrong but the payday that came after. You could earn in one day what took others two months. It was the reason why so many found their way back into prison. Some didn't even try. For him it was meant to be different. Jack took a swig of his drink and the phone rang.

Billy glanced down. "It's Ronny."

"Told you."

It was a given that he would call back. They always did.

Billy tapped accept and Ronny was the first to speak. "Tomorrow morning, first thing at ten. You come alone. Bring the cash and head north on Lee Road. You are going to pass over the Bogue Falaya. The first turn on the left will lead you up to a house. Meet me there."

With that he hung up.

Billy put out his cigarette and Jack's eyebrow went up.

"Now how do you suppose we do this?" Billy asked.

"Leave that to me."

A TV was playing in the background with the volume down. Jack turned and saw it flip to the news channel. A jolt of panic flooded his being when he saw Billy's and his mug shot along with a photo of Ruby come up on the screen. It probably didn't help that one of the old-timers at the bar glanced up then swiveled in his chair. Jack gave Billy a slight kick under the table.

"What?"

He jerked his head towards the TV. Billy's eyes flitted up and then he looked at the guy who was now speaking with his pal beside him. For a few brief seconds both of them looked at each other until they heard the sound of a gun being cocked. The bartender had reached under the counter and brought out a large double-barrel shotgun.

Billy was already half out of his seat when Henry spoke.

"Stay right where you are."

"No, Henry, you know me."

"I know you are a crook."

Jack remained calm and collected. These kind of things didn't usually go south if no one made any hasty moves.

"We don't have any kid. This is a mistake."

"Then you won't mind sticking around and telling the cops that. Wiley, get on the phone."

One of the guys on the stools hopped down and was heading over to a phone when Billy rose to his feet.

"Billy. I'm warning you. I don't want to do it but I will."

Jack was slightly out of view in the booth. He could see all of this playing out in the mirrors on the walls. His hand reached behind his back and pulled his Glock. He squeezed the grip tightly. This was the worst kind of situation he could find himself in. He didn't want to kill anyone in here. They were good people. Hard-working. Just folk trying to do what was right.

"Now, Henry, how long have I been coming in here?"

Billy's gun was hanging down in his hand beside his leg. For all his attempts to negotiate it was doing little to alleviate this guy's fears. In the mirror Jack could see the other guy reach the phone behind the counter. He couldn't let him make that call. This wasn't going to end well for anyone. Billy was edging his way forward hoping to get closer to Henry when the shotgun went off and blew a hole in the wall.

Billy ducked down instinctively.

"The next one goes in you."

"Fuck, Henry. My old man knew you, so did my brothers. Look, the kid on the screen is my daughter." He paused. Jack hadn't taken his eyes off the man who was by the phone. He hadn't placed the call. The noise from the gun had startled him. His hand was hovering over it.

"Go ahead and make that call, Wiley," Henry repeated.

Wiley looked as if he had pissed himself with fright. He had to have been at least eighty years of age.

"Henry, c'mon now. I don't want you to get hurt."

That only riled him up more. "You come into my bar and threaten me?"

"Whoa, whoa, I didn't say that. I just meant you're holding a gun and…"

Negotiating wasn't getting them anywhere. Jack watched as Wiley picked up the phone. Henry's full attention was on Billy. In his mind all he was thinking was, *put the gun down. Just put it down.* But he wasn't going to do it.

Jack wheeled his Glock up in one smooth motion around the edge of the booth. Before Henry could aim at him, a bullet hit him in the shoulder sending him crashing back into his bar. His finger must have been on the trigger as the shotgun fired in the air. Billy didn't waste a second racing over to the old guy by the phone. He didn't need to tell him what to do, he'd already dropped the phone in fear.

Jack got up and went around the counter to check on Henry. He was still alive. He'd been hit in the right shoulder. "Billy, get me some cloth and bring the phone here."

He turned toward the old guy and added, "Sorry, old-timer. But he's telling you the truth. We don't have her."

The very words cut him to the core. If they didn't have her, who did?

He patched up Henry as best as he could, called an ambulance and then both of them got the hell out of there.

Chapter 26

She stared down at the bloody hole in the man's forehead. Isabel was exhausted. By now she should have been tucked away in bed, but this didn't look like it was going to be one of those nights.

She'd been on site at the Sunrise Motel for the past twenty minutes talking to a witness who said she had seen a man leave the motel with a girl that matched the description from the Amber Alert. By now she already had a grainy photo of the guy from the hospital incident. It was pathetic. She pulled it up on her phone and showed it to the woman who was as thin as a rake.

"Hard to tell, it was kind of dark. I just remember seeing them come in. The girl didn't look happy."

Now, as police examined the body inside the registration office, she wondered why anyone would want to take Jack's daughter. Better still, why keep her alive and hole up in a motel? Perhaps he wasn't anything to do with Jack. She was fifty minutes away from the hospital in New Orleans. She wanted to talk to Theresa again. She was certain that she was holding back key information that might help but it was late and her last conversation with Theresa hadn't exactly gone well. She was still conflicted about whether to have her charged for assisting Jack.

"Any luck?" she asked another officer who came into the room.

"We are stopping traffic but nothing so far."

They had set up a small perimeter around the city on the main roads and were stopping vehicles. It was the best they could do right now. Isabel rubbed her eyes feeling a wave of tiredness. For what she got paid, she often wondered why she continued doing the job. But it was in her blood. She couldn't imagine herself doing anything else. Besides, just remembering her father's death at the hands of a home invader gave her more than enough fuel to keep going.

About ten minutes later an officer approached her to

let her know that they had received a call about a shooting down at a local bar on the west side.

"Bartender says Jack Winchester and Billy were in there."

"Let's go." Isabel didn't waste another second, she hopped into her car and followed a cruiser across town. The fact that he was still in town, and in a bar of all places, meant he couldn't have been worried about getting caught.

Police lights lit up the dark streets that were practically empty. Covington was vastly different to New Orleans. A small town with a population of just under ten thousand, it was just far enough north that it missed Hurricane Katrina when it made landfall. Many of the people who had lost their homes had moved to Covington and since 2005 it had become one of the many cities in the area that had seen a lot of growth.

Rain beat against her windshield. The wipers couldn't move fast enough. It was the beginning of Hurricane Danielle. Trees swayed and bent in the harsh ninety-mile-an-hour winds. By the time she reached the bar, the roads were being turned into a shallow flowing stream. Water gushed from the drains and gutters overflowed.

Isabel pulled her coat up around her ears as the rain plastered her hair to her face. She double-timed it across the sidewalk and ducked under the yellow police tape. Inside, the witnesses were still on scene.

"What have we got here?"

"Bartender is at the hospital for a gunshot wound to the shoulder. These guys saw it all."

Isabel went over and introduced herself. They looked old, pale and shaken up by what had taken place.

"You want to take me through what happened?"

"I just told him twice."

"Humor me."

The old man's hands were shaking. He took a sip of a double scotch that was on the counter.

"We come here all the time. We'd seen Billy Dixon before but not the other fella. Henry had his gun on them and asked me to call you guys. Which reminds me. That damn ambulance took forever. I thought we were going to lose a friend."

"Who shot him? The other guy, Jack Winchester?"

He shrugged. "If that's his name."

She held up a photo of him.

"That's the man."

"Did he say anything before he left?"

"Yeah, he said they didn't have the girl and that the police had it all wrong."

Isabel thought back to the man in the hospital. To what Theresa had said about her attackers. Had they taken the girl as retribution? If they had and Jack knew about it, this was about to turn ugly real fast.

Under the direction of the witnesses she went over to the booth to see if there was anything they had left behind. She shook her head. No luck. She was still waiting to hear back from the police on whether or not they had found out what hotel he was staying at in New Orleans. She'd asked the sergeant on duty to contact motels in the area in the hope that they could find him or the other assailant, but that was going to take a while.

Time was against her. Whatever reasons he might have had for leaving would be tossed to the wind now that he knew about his daughter being taken. Her mind went back to the bloodbath at the club in L.A. She sure as hell didn't want that to happen again.

She was about to leave when her phone rang. It was Theresa.

"Agent Baker, is it true?"

"I'm afraid so."

Then it dawned on her. Might have Jack thought that this was just a ploy to get him to turn himself in? A setup by the police to lure him out?

She heard Theresa sobbing hard on the other end of the line. "Who's taken her?" she managed to say between sobs.

"We're not sure yet."

"Carla?"

Isabel went quiet. Thankfully she didn't need to explain. Her silence was an answer in itself. "Where's

Billy? Jack?"

"We're trying to find them but with the storm coming in, the visibility out there is pretty bad. Hopefully by morning we'll have a lead and I will let you know immediately."

"Morning?" she stammered. "She'll be dead by morning. If it's the same men that..."

"Theresa, we don't know that yet. The sighting we've had places her here in Covington with one male suspect."

"Perhaps it's Jack?"

She didn't want to lie to her but at the same time it wasn't going to do her any good to fret over this. There was very little they could do. Everything that could be done was being done.

"It's very possible," she replied knowing full well that it wasn't Jack or Billy.

In between the loud cries, Isabel tried to get her to calm down. "Theresa, do you know anywhere Billy might go? Anyone he knows?"

"I... I don't."

"Think. Right now we have very little to go on."

"Um, there was a guy by the name of Mike. That he used to have around from time to time. I'm just trying to think of where he said he lived."

An officer across the room motioned for Isabel.

"Call me back, okay?"

"Yeah. Yeah."

She hung up and went over to the officer in charge. "Seems the bar had some surveillance footage."

He led her out back to a screen. On a small flat-screen TV, black-and-white images came up that showed the outside and the inside of the bar.

"Go back."

One camera was angled down across the booths, and one towards the door. Another was out the front and another focused on the rear door. An officer went back until the images of Jack and Billy came up.

"That's it. Play it from there."

In a second-by-second playback she watched what happened. She saw Jack pull his gun and wait. What are you waiting for? Why didn't you kill them? Her eyes scanned the different people including the old witness who was standing by the phone. Then she watched him take the shot.

"He could have killed him but he didn't."

"Bad shot?"

"No. Not this guy."

Then she saw the smartphone on the table. "Go back a bit further."

She watched Billy talk on the phone then lay it down. The phone screen lit up again about five minutes later.

"Pause it. You think you can zoom in on that?"

"Agent, this is Radio Shack crap that we are dealing with. Maybe if we took this down to the station, we might be able to."

She could feel frustration building. Give me a break, she thought.

"Alright, see what you can do."

The officer showed her a few streams from the outside but it was useless. They disappeared into the shadows.

There was very little else that could be done. It was getting close to midnight by the time Isabel booked into a local Holiday Inn. It was the first one she saw. She didn't care what the bed was like. She knew the moment her head hit that pillow she'd be gone.

As she closed the door behind her, she leaned up against it and slipped down to the floor. Isabel wrapped her arms around her legs and rested her head on her knees. It was hard to turn off the mind. It kept replaying the events in the hospital. She could still hear the sound of gunfire and screams.

After taking a quick shower she was about to slip into bed when her phone vibrated on the side table. It was Cooper. She hit accept and slumped back onto the bed.

"I hear things are heating up. Amber Alert. Multiple shootings."

"Yeah, it's..." she trailed off not really knowing what to say about it all. To be honest it was all getting away from her and she felt like a donkey trying to bite a carrot that was hanging from a stick in front of her.

"That's why I should have been there."

Here we go, she thought. She smirked. Regardless of what a bonehead he was at times, she kind of missed having him with her.

"Yeah, you would have this case wrapped up by now."

"In the bag," he replied and they both chuckled a little. Outside the storm was getting worse. No doubt the police would have ceased stopping vehicles in this weather. She heard what sounded like a stick hit the window. A flash of lighting and she saw that it was tree branches. They looked like gnarled fingers as they raked at her window.

Chapter 27

Neither of them slept much that night. It wasn't the fact that Ruby was on both of their minds. It was the storm. Within a matter of hours of leaving the bar it had gone from mild to extreme. By morning the storm had still not let up. Jack stood by the window in a motel, two towns over. Billy was paranoid the police were going to show up.

"I can't go back. I won't," he'd said multiple times that night. He was beginning to sound a lot like Jack. There was something to be said about doing time. Once out, you didn't want to feel trapped again. And right now both of them were beginning to feel like hedged-in animals on a safari hunt. They had taken turns that night to keep an eye out for police. None showed up but then no one would have been stupid enough to go out in that weather. The entire room shook as violent winds whipped against the door and windows, threatening to break them wide open.

It was a little after eight in the morning. Outside Jack could see store signs that had been torn from the ground and scattered across the parking lot. The wooden fence that wrapped around the pool had been ripped apart and scattered. Small trees had been uprooted and garbage tumbled across the ground.

"You know he's probably not even got the meth."

"Yeah, I know. But it doesn't matter. Just stay cool."

Billy fired up a cigarette and peeked out the side of the curtain. "What I wouldn't do for a fix."

Jack studied him. His hands were shaking as he took a deep pull.

"Theresa knows."

"What?"

"That you're using again."

"How the f—" His eyes dropped and then met Jack's. "Fuck's sake."

"What, did you think you could hide it from her?"

"No. I wasn't going to keep doing it. It was a reaction

to what happened to her. I just needed a little something to take the edge off, you know."

"No. I don't. You can't do that shit around Ruby."

"Yeah, well, I might not have to worry about that."

Jack grabbed a hold of him.

"I swear. If anything happens to her. I'm going to…"

"Get off, man. That might work where you come from. But around here everyone threatens."

"I don't threaten."

Billy studied him for a second then walked away in a huff. He picked up his phone and glanced at it for the ninth time that morning.

Jack frowned. "You expecting to hear from someone?"

"Theresa. She's bound to find out about Ruby from the news. She hasn't called."

"That's because she has learned already. She won't call."

"Oh yeah?"

"Trust me on this one."

Jack glanced at the clock, went over to the coffee

machine and tore the corner off a bag of coffee. He poured the grinds into the filter and put it on.

"You said you were from New York. What did you do there?"

Jack didn't reply. "Just get your shit together, we are going to head out soon."

"I'm just trying to be friendly."

Jack snorted. *Maybe if you hadn't fucked up we wouldn't be here now,* Jack thought.

The fact was, no matter where he went, trouble might be found. But this was a whole new level of trouble. Seeing his mug shot on an Amber Alert meant they were not only under the watchful eye of the police and FBI but now the general public would be looking out for them. At this rate the only way he'd be able to escape his past would be to leave the country. But with no passport that was out of the question.

After downing an awful-tasting cup of coffee, they slipped out and drove north. As they were expecting Billy to show up alone, Jack laid in the trunk. Being two towns over they were a good forty minutes away from their destination. The wind whipped against the car making it difficult to drive. The sun was hidden behind dark clouds. The grey skies only made him feel worse. Everything in him wanted to go searching for Ruby but he had no idea where she was or even where to begin.

Had they taken her early in the event that Billy didn't pay? It was possible. People were prone to get cold feet at the last minute and try to duck out from debts they owed. It wouldn't have been the first time he'd seen criminals swoop in before payment was made. It was like insurance to them.

As they got closer, Billy pulled over to the side of the road and took a piss. He banged the trunk before he got back in to let Jack know they were getting close. He continued driving for another ten minutes, before he brought the car down to a crawl and made a sharp left off the main road down onto a gravel trail.

The car came to a halt and Jack could hear voices outside. The door slammed and the suspension gave way.

Voices outside were muffled but Jack caught the gist of the conversation. Footsteps moved around to the rear of the car. A key was inserted into the back. Jack readied himself.

The lid on the trunk popped up and that's when it all went south on him. Four guys were holding shotguns at him.

"Get him out of there."

Billy stood back. "Sorry, Jack, but I've far more to lose than you."

"You bastard," he said through gritted teeth.

It didn't take them long to zip tie Jack.

"Someone offered me a tidy little price if I handed you over to them."

"Who?"

"You'll see."

As two guys strong-armed him away, he glanced back to see Billy slapping hands and pulling the guy he assumed was Ronny into him for a shoulder hug.

"How you doing, man?"

"Oh, it's been a while."

The two men led him into the house. Inside he glanced around at the bags of meth stacked against the wall. Out the corner of his eye he noticed several females in the room partially naked snorting up crystal while one guy was getting head in the corner. Jack was led down into a dark basement and placed in a chair with his arms behind his back. One of them covered his eyes and shoved another piece of material into his mouth. It tasted like oil. It was damp and the whole place stunk of urine.

He couldn't see what they were doing but he could feel them zip tying his ankles to the chair. A few seconds later the sound of boots pounding against wooden steps, then a door slamming shut and several bolts being slotted into place.

In the darkness he ground his teeth against the material. In an attempt to get out he began shifting his body but they'd bound him tightly. Frustration soon turned to anger. He became quiet to hear the conversation that was going on upstairs. Footsteps clattered against the hardwood floors.

"You had me worried for a minute, I thought Mike's crew had taken it."

Laughter ensued and then the clinking of bottles.

"After today we are going to be fucking made."

"You bet."

What the hell had Billy got himself involved in now? And how the hell was he going to get out of this? His blood boiled at the thought that someone had his daughter, and that in an attempt to do the right thing he now found himself blindsided by Theresa's lunatic boyfriend.

Chapter 28

It was the break she had been hoping to get. Isabel received the call some time in the early hours of the morning from the Covington Police Department. Apparently Billy Dixon had phoned the police several hours after the incident in the bar. He hadn't got through to her but had given the police a message to let them know that if they wanted Jack Winchester, they should be ready for a phone call sometime after noon. That was it. The officer who took the call said he hung up after leaving the message. He thought it was a joke, someone who had seen the Amber Alert and was playing games with the police. It happened. All manner of people would step forward and send the police on a wild goose chase. But right now it was the one thing she had to go on.

Isabel left her phone on speakerphone while she got ready.

"Run that by me again. He said Winchester took

him?"

"Seems that way."

"So how did he manage to make that call?"

"Who knows, Cooper? All I care about is getting this asshole behind bars."

"What are you going to do when this is over?"

"Return to Florida."

"What about New York?"

"Are you kidding? That grimy place. I need the ocean, sunshine and folks who don't grunt when you ask them for help."

That morning she hurried. She was about ready to bring this to a close. The thought of returning to Florida and putting this all behind her seemed almost too good to be true. But she was still no closer to knowing where Theresa's daughter was.

* * *

Giovanni had seen Winchester's mug shot on the news the previous night. He knew it would only be a matter of time before the police caught up with him. He sat sipping coffee. He'd been out briefly that morning to pick up some breakfast for the kid and himself. His mind circled back and forth on what to do next. He kind of figured they would put out an Amber Alert and that would prevent Winchester from leaving but he still had no idea where he was. The aftermath of the storm meant that the streets were filled with workers trying to get power up in some areas of the town. It had been one hell of a night. He set his coffee down and grabbed up a packet of cigarettes. He lit one and the kid stared at him.

"What are you looking at?"

"You shouldn't smoke."

"I shouldn't do a lot of things. Eat up your breakfast."

He continued flipping through channels until he came across a local news channel broadcasting a report about a shooting down at a local bar. They had tied it to the two men wanted in the Amber Alert. So far they had nothing on the whereabouts of the kid. That was good news.

Giovanni got up and went over to the window. He glanced outside and then back at the kid. He was beginning to second-guess his decision to take her. What was he thinking? Without a lead on where Jack was, or a means to contact him, he had nothing.

* * *

Jack heard the door unlock. He'd been down in the basement for what seemed like an hour, maybe two. Footsteps approached and then the rag in his mouth was taken out along with the material around his eyes. Standing in front of him was Billy Dixon.

"Brought you some food, thought you might be hungry being as we didn't have breakfast."

"What are you playing at?"

Billy studied him and then set the plate down. He paced up and down a bit, cast a nervous glance upstairs and then took a seat across from him.

"I'm handling the problem like I told you I would."

"You already knew them, didn't you?"

He cocked his head to one side and smirked. "I didn't know initially they were the ones who took the meth until fat boy mentioned his name, but yeah, I know Ronny.

We go way back. Unlike Mike, Ronny doesn't have the connections I do. So we've made a little arrangement. He'll get far more money selling to the big guys than trying to distribute this on the streets."

"Who did you make the deal with?"

He breathed in deeply. "It dawned on me last night after we got out of the bar. The cops are looking for you and me. Now, I can understand them coming after me because they would think I took Ruby but you? You've got to have done something bad to piss them off. So I made a call to the cops. I said I was being held by you and that I would arrange for them to come and collect with the assurance that no charges were laid against me from the bar incident."

"You asshole."

"As for Tex. Well, I just got off the phone with his son Kalen. Him and his crew are going to meet with us this morning and arrange a little deal whereby my debt is cleared and we make a tidy profit."

Jack shook his head.

"I told you. I would handle this."

"You have just signed your death sentence."

Billy frowned confused.

"How so? By you? You're the one tied up."

"No, by Tex's men, you idiot."

Again he looked completely stumped by what Jack was saying. That's because he didn't know how these things worked. The moment Billy had told him about what Tex had done to others who had overstepped the line, he knew he was dealing with a man much like Gafino. He didn't care about the money that Billy owed. It was all about watching him sweat. The torture had already begun, the second they cut him loose and gave him forty-eight hours. Whether he returned with the money or not they would hunt him down, bring him in and make a spectacle out of him. They would use him to set another example to others. To send out a clear message that it didn't matter who they were, no one was immune.

"Tex is going to be more than happy. He's going to get far more than forty thousand. So are we."

"If you want to live, you need to get me out of here."

"You just hang tight. This will all be over real soon."

Before Jack could say another word, Billy shoved the rag back in his mouth and covered his eyes. Jack knew he had to get out of there. Once Tex's men showed up, things were going to go from bad to worse real fast. He rocked back and forth hoping to break the wooden chair that he was on. His ankles were tied to the legs and his wrists bound behind his back and attached to the chair. Going by memory of what he saw around him, he knew there was a table behind him. The floor was concrete and there were metal support pillars for the floors above. If he could just get over to one of those he might be able to use the corner of the metal to cut through the plastic zip tie. Jack rocked back and forth trying to get some momentum going. When the chair collapsed against the floor it took the wind out of him. Still attached, his binds bit into his skin. This wasn't going to be easy.

Chapter 29

Kalen had eight of his men gear up. Billy must have a been a complete idiot to think that he could try to sell back product that belonged to his father. As he listened to him on the phone he just played along with it.

"So you are going to pay back the forty grand in product?"

"That's right, plus you can tell Tex that I will throw in an extra twenty grand just as my way of apologizing for the inconvenience."

"I must say that's very generous of you." Kalen glanced at one of his men and he smirked.

"Well, I know that we have had a good working relationship and I just want to make sure that is maintained."

"And how did you manage to come up with that much product so fast?"

"Contacts. You know me, Kalen, I've always got

someone in my back pocket."

"By the way, word on the street is that Mike hasn't been seen. You wouldn't know anything about that?"

"Oh you know, Mike. He goes off the grid quite frequently on benders. He's probably partying in Vegas right now. Anyway, why's that?"

"Because he worked for us."

Kalen waited to hear his reply. He almost felt like bursting out laughing. Billy cleared his throat. "He worked for you? But I thought he was solo. Heck, he said he was solo."

"So you have spoken to him?"

"Uh. Well, yeah. I mean, we are old buddies. He said he was creating product himself. He was raving about his new cook."

"You mean, our new cook."

"No. he didn't say that. Hell, I even warned him that he needed to be careful, you know with cooking and selling on the streets."

"Because of my father?"

Billy became tongue-tied as he tried to talk his way of the hole he was digging.

"I told him that only those who distribute for Tex are…"

He trailed off and Kalen let out a chuckle. He didn't want to spook him and cause him to run. Right now he wanted to get his hands on the product and on Billy.

"I'm pulling your leg, Billy. Relax. It's cool. I know there are distributors who aren't working for my father. And hell, I don't give a shit about Mike. He was an asshole. It's just he owed us a good amount of money."

"Perhaps he did a runner."

"Yeah. Maybe." He paused. "So when and where do you want to meet?"

"You know Lee Road? There's a house by the water. The first on the left after the bridge. I'm thinking you could swing by here around about two?"

"We'll be there. And Billy, you better have the product as time is up."

He let out a nervous laugh. "Oh don't worry, I've got

more than enough for Tex. Um, before you go. Do you guys have my daughter Ruby?"

"No. Why would we have her?"

"Well, I thought that maybe you had picked her up. You know, until I came up with the money."

"We don't have her. Speak to you later, Billy."

With that Kalen hung up. He looked at one of his men who was also a friend of his. "Get hold of my father, let him know that we have a meeting arranged, then get the boys together. We are heading out in the next half an hour."

"Didn't he say two o'clock?"

"Yeah. We're going in early."

* * *

Down at the police department that morning the place was a hive of activity. For a small department this had been the most action they had seen in several years. Isabel had updated Simon on what was about to go down. He had arranged to have four FBI agents to assist with the apprehension of Winchester. They would arrive within the hour. Covington had their SWAT team getting ready.

"We will be blocking off the roads in an eight-mile radius around the house. We'll have eyes in the sky."

"What about the weather?" another officer asked. A murmur spread throughout the group. People were aware of the danger. Evacuation orders had already been given to those in the New Orleans area as Hurricane Danielle still wasn't over. Almost like the tide, it was as though the storm had pulled back for a period of time to allow itself to build up for one final crescendo.

"Yeah, boss, it's pretty bad out there."

"Right now this is what we have in place. We can only control what is within our control."

"They don't pay me enough to deal with this shit," one of them muttered. The sergeant on duty asked who said that but none of them spoke up and none of them pointed the finger. It was the way they were. They watched out for each other and none of them wanted to be out in this weather. Isabel glanced outside. The light morning rain had turned into a heavy downpour making visibility limited.

"Now, this is Agent Baker. Most of you have met her; she will be heading up the raid today. Do you care to add anything?"

She did but in a room full of this much testosterone, and the way the weather was outside, she didn't think anything she added would make them feel any better about this. By all accounts this was going to be a simple bust. In and out.

Isabel had downed four cups of coffee by the time the phone call came in from Billy. She was handed the phone by an officer. They placed the call on speakerphone so all the guys in the room could hear.

"Do you have the girl, Billy?"

"No, I already told the officer yesterday. We don't have her. Listen up."

He gave the address for the place and wanted to make sure that she came alone.

"You have my word on that."

"If he even gets the slightest inkling that you are with

anyone else this shit is going to go south. Now do I have your word?"

"You have it."

"Noon."

With that he hung up.

"Alright guys, load up and let's move out."

Chapter 30

Water poured over the gutters creating a mini waterfall as Billy stepped out onto the porch to have a cigarette. The Bogue Falaya River had risen up to the edge of the bank. The ground either side had turned into slick mud that was flowing into the dark water. Ronny joined him outside with a beer in his hand.

"Are you sure about this?"

"They are going to take me in. All you have to do is get the money from Kalen and give him the product. Trust me, I've done countless deals with these guys. Just keep your men in line. If they get a sense you are playing them they will cut you down before you've had a chance to swallow."

"And the guy downstairs?"

"They'll take him with me."

Ronny nodded and took a swig of his drink. Billy was worried. He'd worked with Ronny countless times in the past. They'd grown up together. Both of them came from the same neighborhood and had experienced their own share of run-ins with the law. It didn't take long for them to get into trouble. Back then it was stealing cars. The first one they stole they sold for two hundred bucks to a guy who ran a wrecker's. He would spray-paint them and resell them. Eventually it became a constant means of getting enough money to get the attention of women. Most of the time they would spend what they earned on booze and drugs.

Of course it didn't take long before they shifted up to dealing narcotics on the streets. At first it was simple stuff like marijuana. They had their own little grow operation that they ran out of a friend's garage.

Soon both of them began to dabble in meth using the shake and bake method. At first it was just an additional source of revenue but before long they were making more money from that than they were from marijuana. They couldn't make it fast enough.

Then Tex started clamping down on small operations.

Even though they got less money, it meant the chances of being busted by police or killed by him were less.

"Are you sure they are going to let you go?"

"I haven't done anything. They have no reason to hold me."

"But your record, man."

"I've done my time."

Ronny took a deep puff from his blunt. Ronny was a strange-looking guy who had long black hair that was slightly curly. He looked as if he had just stepped out of an '80s soft rock band. Whenever he didn't have a bottle of beer in his hand, he was smoking blunts.

"So what's the deal with your little girl? I saw her face plastered all over the news."

"I don't know where she is. To be quite honest, she was a little shit half the time so whoever has got her has done me a favor."

"What are you going to do with your share after?"

"I'm taking Theresa out of here. Maybe go to the Bahamas, get a little shack down there and open my own bar. I need a slower pace of life."

"I hear you, man. We aren't getting any younger."

And that was the truth. Billy was getting close to forty and all he had to show for his life was a record of criminal behavior, a house that belonged to Theresa and a shitty trailer. He'd always imagined that by the time he made it to forty he would be set up in some nice crib in the city with a couple of kids of his own and a business that operated twenty-four seven without him being involved. Of course he would look in on it from time to time but that would be all. He'd always been averse to work; at least any work that didn't pay well.

As they sat out there watching Mother Nature do its worst, a silver SUV came into the driveway followed by a black sedan. Gravel crunched and large puddles splashed. Billy squinted. Who the hell was that? As the vehicles got closer his eyes widened.

"Shit!"

"What?"

"It's Kalen."

Billy glanced at his watch, it was nearly noon.

"What the hell's he doing here? It's not two."

"I don't know but get the guys and product ready."

Ronny went inside while Billy stood to his feet. He couldn't believe Kalen was here right now. He gave a fake smile as they pulled up close to the house. Kalen was the first to get out, then his men came around. They dashed to get under the cover of the porch.

"What are you doing here so early?"

"Change of plans. You got the product?"

Billy eyed the men. Each of them carried a semi-automatic rifle. "I don't think you'll need those."

"Precaution. I think you understand."

Billy called out to Ronny while keeping his eye on the men. He glanced past Kalen.

"You expecting someone?"

"No. I thought I saw another car."

"Come, let's take a seat."

Kalen wrapped his arm around Billy and led him over to the porch rocker.

"So tell me again, how did you manage to get so much product in forty-eight hours?"

"I had a friend of mine who owed me a favor."

"Owed a favor. Do I know him?"

"No. No, I don't think you do."

"Forty grand in meth is a lot. Is he distributing locally?"

"He was. He's out of the business now."

Billy swallowed hard. His pulse was racing and he was sweating a little. Kalen ran his tongue around the inside of his own teeth before lighting a cigarette and blowing out smoke.

"Your friend. He got a name?"

"Ah, you wouldn't know him."

Kalen raised his eyebrows. "You would be surprised how many dealers we know."

"Markus."

"Markus." Kalen nodded. "Markus…"

"Tomlin."

Kalen shouted over to his buddy. "You heard of a

Markus Tomlin?"

"I don't believe I have, boss."

Ronny came out and glanced at the others. He brought a bag of meth with him and handed it off to Kalen who examined it.

"Mind if I test the goods?"

"No. Go ahead," Ronny said.

"What's your name?" Kalen asked him.

"Ronny."

Kalen reached down to his leg and pulled out a knife from a sheath. He laid the bag on the table and jabbed the knife in, splitting it wide open. He cupped the product and took some out before taking the back of the knife and smashing up the chunks into a fine powder in front of him.

"Ronny, come around here so you can block the wind a little."

Some of the powder was getting blown off the table.

"That's a good lad. Alright, go ahead and snort it."

Ronny's eyes darted between Billy and Kalen.

"What?"

"Snort it."

"I don't…"

"You want to sell this? Then go ahead and fucking snort it."

"I thought you were going to test it."

"I am. By having you snort it. What? You think I'm going to snort that shit up my nose?"

Billy could tell that Ronny was nervous. He'd never been the kind of guy to deal with confrontations. He was an opportunist. A thief and a damn fine one at that. Billy gestured to him to go ahead.

Ronny went to scoop up some.

"No, come on down here."

Again he gave a look of confusion but then dropped down to one knee to place his nose against the product and snort it up. Kalen watched carefully, a smirk dancing on his lips as the product vanished up Ronny's nose. His eyes rolled back a bit before he got this wide grin on his face.

"And the next line."

"What?"

"I want to see you do the next line."

"But this stuff is potent."

"That's what I want to see. I don't know how potent it is."

Ronny rubbed his nose and then did the next line. Now he had a look on his face as if he had just stepped into heaven itself.

"Oooh, you missed a bit."

Kalen pointed to a small amount of powder at the edge of the table.

"Go on. Finish it off."

This time as Ronny placed his nose against the table, Kalen grabbed his head and held it against the table. Ronny's face was turned on its side with one ear facing up.

"Shit, man, what are you doing?" Billy said rising to his feet only to be told to sit back down by Kalen's men who had their guns on them.

"How's that product? Is it good?"

"Yeah. Yeah. It's good."

"It should be. It's fucking ours!" Kalen shouted just before he jammed a knife down into the side of Ronny's head. It went right through his ear and penetrated deep into the skull. Ronny let out this high-pitched scream. Kalen held him there as blood poured out all over the table. Ronny's four guys came out with guns but were quickly told to put them down by Kalen's men. After seeing what he'd done to Ronny, they didn't argue. Who would? Ronny's guys were just youngsters in their early twenties. None of them had done time. They all thought they were big men when trouble wasn't knocking on their door. Now they looked as if they were going to piss themselves in fear.

Kalen pushed the knife until it couldn't go any further before he stood up and placed his foot against Ronny's face so he could pull it back out. Ronny's lifeless body slumped to the floor.

"Did you really think we would buy your story about a

friend owing you a favor? No one would cough up that amount of product as a favor. You must be the biggest fucking idiot I have ever met."

Kalen reached over and grabbed a hold of Billy by the head.

"Now I should fucking kill you right here and now, but my father wants me to bring you in alive."

"Please, Kalen, I…"

"Shut the fuck up, you sniveling punk. You thought you were going to sell back to us, our own product?"

"I didn't know it was yours. I swear."

"And that whole shit about Mike going to Vegas." He turned back and looked at his men. "You stupid fuck."

Billy's heart was racing.

"Time is up, Billy."

He'd just muttered the words when several police cruisers came skidding into view. Doors opened and guns were raised. Kalen's men turned and opened fire. The noise was deafening. Between the rain, wind and sloshing of the river, which had gone wild, the sound of gunfire erupting and men ducking for cover was overwhelming. Kalen released his grip on Billy and he fell to the floor.

"You set us up!"

Billy didn't even get a chance to speak. Kalen pulled the trigger and fired two rounds into him.

Chapter 31

The eye in the sky had seen the activity and radioed it in long before Isabel and SWAT showed up. She was en route to the house when she was told to hold back. They had identified several men holding rifles. The police would send in SWAT. Something that she didn't want to do but it was out of her hands now. She was now playing second fiddle to what they wanted.

All she could think about was Jack Winchester making a break for it.

"Tell them to stand down."

"It's too late for that, they've opened fire," the officer in charge repeated over her ear mic. "Hold back until it's safe."

"Hold back. The hell I will."

Isabel blew into the driveway in her sedan. The wet ground below the tires nearly made her lose control of the vehicle. The first thing she saw was multiple assailants.

The next was her car along with the cruisers being riddled with bullets. Metal pinged and glass shattered as she ducked down and forced her car door open. She slipped into wet mud that felt alive.

Officers off to her left were yelling and taking cover behind their vehicles as they returned fire. Crawling on the ground in the thick mud she made it to the edge of her car tire and glanced beyond it. She aimed her Glock and fired, but from her position, it was useless. With the sheer amount of rain coming down, and too many cars in the way, she was more likely to die from being hit by lightning than by a bullet. It was complete pandemonium. The forest hedged them in on the right-hand side, while the river threatened on the left. Staying low to the ground she moved her way through the mud and slid down the embankment so that she could go around the side of the house. The river was rushing hard, curling up large amounts of dark water that smashed down over the edge. Every step through the brush felt treacherous. One misstep and she would be in the river and taken down by the strong current.

The gunfire didn't let up as she tried to stay out of view of the gunmen who were positioned at various places along the porch and behind their vehicles.

* * *

Jack was still struggling to get out of his restraints when he heard gunfire. That was followed by the sound of a chopper overhead and boots clattering above him. Enveloped by the darkness of the rag around his eyes he pressed his head against the floor and scraped it back and forth until he could see a small amount of light from underneath. There was no telling what the hell was going on up there except that it probably was related to that idiot Billy.

As hard as he tried to free himself, it was useless. The binds cut into his wrists. They had fastened him so tight that unless he broke the chair itself he wouldn't be getting out.

* * *

Isabel shuffled through the cluster of trees and

undergrowth towards the side of the house. She slipped several times and found herself inches away from the edge of the water. Her clothing was covered in a thick layer of mud. Lots of it was in her hair and on her face. When she got closer to the back of the house, a younger guy not much older than twenty-one came rushing out the back. He wasn't even looking where he was going until it was too late. Isabel took him down and laid her knee on the back of his neck. She looked up to make sure no one else was coming out.

"Where's Jack Winchester?"

"Get the fuck off."

She pressed harder. She was in no mood for taking shit.

"Where is he?"

"I don't know who the hell you are on about."

"Billy Dixon?"

"He's dead. They shot him."

"The guy who he was with?"

"In the basement."

She would have used her cuffs on the guy but she needed those for Winchester. Instead, she got off him, took his gun and let him go. He was a small pawn in the game she was playing. The kid rushed off in a state of panic. There was no way in hell she was going to lose Winchester. She pulled up to the back of the house and peeked through the door. Several men were inside. All of them were packing heat and firing rounds out the front. Slipping down around the side of the house, she moved along until she came across a small window. Down on her knees she rubbed her palm across the pane of glass to clear the dirt and cobwebs away. It didn't help much. Her hands were covered in dirt. Peering in she spotted him. Laid on his side, tied up and unable to move, he wasn't going anywhere.

She was getting up when a bullet struck her in the shoulder.

"Fucking pig," A guy had come darting around the side to escape. If it hadn't been for the fact that she had fallen back into thick brush, she was certain he would have killed her. He was firing rounds rapidly at the ground. She looked up and couldn't see him, which meant he had no idea where she was. As she circled around a boulder and he came back into view, she returned fire bringing him down in six shots. She unloaded the magazine and slammed another one into place as she approached the house. Gunshot wound or not, she wasn't going to let Winchester go.

By now several other officers had circled around and came up on her. They checked her wound briefly before taking fire. They might have tied a cloth around it but bullets were flying all over the place.

"Ma'am, I'll lead you back," one said.

"To hell you will, I'm here to get Winchester."

With pain coursing through her body from the wound to her shoulder she pressed on towards the back of the house. The officer persisted and told her she needed to go back. She was losing too much blood. At the back door, the officer, who went by the name Reed, insisted he lead the way. She was sandwiched between him and another officer as they entered. They hadn't been in there more than a few seconds when they were fired upon. Isabel took cover in a room immediately off to her right. It was stacked with boxes, some of which she could tell from the open flaps were filled with bags of meth. The smell inside was atrocious; a mixture of weed, alcohol and urine.

"I need to get to the basement." She peeked around the corner and saw that the basement access was a good ten feet away. Bullets were snapping, and men were yelling. The walls were riddled with holes. Reed held his hand up to indicate when, then pointed for her to move. Scrambling forward she burst out into the corridor and went for the door. With her Glock aimed forward and firing in rapid succession she made it. In the event that anyone rushed out to return fire they would have been taken down by a flurry of bullets zipping through the air. She grabbed the door handle and yanked it open. Within a matter of seconds, she was enveloped in the darkness of the damp basement. Cautiously she came down the stairs with her weapon on the ready. She had only seen Jack through the window but that didn't mean there wasn't anyone watching over him.

When she reached the bottom and cleared the ground floor, she rushed over to Jack and yanked off the rag covering his eyes. Jack's eyes immediately widened.

"Jack Winchester, you are under arrest."

* * *

She began cutting the restraints around his feet first, then took out her handcuffs, locked one on to her wrist and the other onto his before she freed his hands.

"You're bleeding," he muttered noticing very little white on her shirt. Blood had soaked it.

"What?"

"I said you're bleeding."

She glanced at him and for a few seconds they locked eyes. She pulled her Glock and hauled him up to his feet, a task that wasn't easy for a woman of her stature. She led the way up the stairs keeping her Glock out in front of her. The sound of gunfire hadn't let up the entire time she'd been down in the basement. The echo of men's voices and boots pounding the floor filled the air. There was no way of knowing if it was the police or the men who had retreated into the house.

"You know, you'd be better off cutting me loose."

"Shut the hell up."

She peered out the door. She saw an officer down, and a man standing over him firing another shot into his face. A burst of anger and she went to rush out but Jack pulled her back.

"What the hell are you doing?" she yelled.

"Saving your ass."

With a flood of indignation, Isabel turned back to the door and yanked him out while firing at the man who was now at the main door. Two rounds hit the guy in the back and he fell to the floor. They turned and retreated towards the rear entrance when another guy came out of the side. Jack plowed his free fist into the guy's face with a right hook, Isabel followed through with a bullet. They took cover in the next room. The curtains were closed leaving them in darkness. She stumbled a little and he caught her.

"You've lost a lot of blood."

"I'm fine," she said straightening up and glancing out down the corridor. Reed, the other officer that she had come in with, was still at the back. He waved her on. She bolted out but at the same time another man came into view further down with an assault rifle. Jack saw it before Isabel did. He threw his body weight onto her, knocking her to the ground. She landed hard. The officer ahead of them fired at the guy but received multiple rounds to his upper torso. When the gunfire stopped, Jack was still laying on top of Isabel. He glanced back to check that the coast was clear. The officer ahead of them was down writhing in agony. Gunfire was still erupting out the front.

"You okay?" he asked her. But she didn't respond. There was a trickle of blood coming from her head. She must have smacked it against the floor on the way down.

Shit! Jack began rooting through her jacket for the key to the handcuffs but another round of gunfire made him reach for her gun instead. He grabbed it up and twisted over just in time. Jack fired one shot and another guy dropped. There was no time to find a key or even a sliver of metal that he could use to push between the teeth. He got up and lifted Isabel up into his arms. Moving fast, he dashed out of the back of the house and kept running towards the tree line. The thought of being hit by a bullet or knocked down to the ground by more cops was at the forefront of his mind the whole time. Branches crunched beneath his boots as he carried her into the thick woodland.

He knew if she didn't get to a hospital soon she would probably die from a loss of blood. When the house was out of sight, he laid her down and fished around in her pockets to find the key.

"C'mon," he muttered while occasionally looking back in the direction of the house. He could hear the sound of the river rushing below. Every pocket he checked was empty. Where the hell had she put it? Perhaps it fell out? *Shit!* he repeated before pummeling the earth with his free

hand. This couldn't get any worse. His daughter had been taken, Billy screwed him over and now he was attached to the wrist of the agent that had a vendetta against him.

Chapter 32

Giovanni had been glued to the screen since a local news channel began streaming back from their eye in the sky. It was hard to tell exactly what was going on but with police and FBI on the scene, he had to wonder if Jack was involved. He glanced at the kid still tied to the bed, she was starting to become a dead weight. He needed to get rid of her fast and yet on the other hand, she was the only leverage he had right now to lure him out.

He paced back and forth.

"I want to go home."

He didn't reply, his mind was ticking over and going through what he could do to find this guy. He needed to get his attention. With the police after them, the chances of Jack searching for his daughter were slim to none. He had to go back to the hospital. There was no way around it. He grabbed up his phone and took a photo of the kid to make sure the mother knew that he wasn't lying.

Before he left he made sure her binds were tight, he didn't want her getting out again.

"I'll be back real soon."

With that he slammed the door behind him and slipped into his car. It would take less than fifty minutes to get to the hospital. There was no telling whether or not they had kept her there or if they had transferred her. Being as he hadn't seen his mug shot on the TV, he was certain that the security cameras hadn't managed to get a clear shot of him. With so much attention focused on the raid and hurricane, security at the hospital would be at a minimum.

Pulling up in the hospital lot, he slipped out and popped open the trunk. In the back he unzipped the case that held the arsenal of weapons. He pulled out two Para Ordnance P18.9's with threaded barrels so that he could attach silencers on both. He removed his jacket and slipped on the leather shoulder holster that was made for both of them. He slipped the guns in and placed his jacket back on. He grabbed up a hunter's knife and slipped it inside his jacket. He hopped back into the car and pulled it up around the back of the hospital by one of the exits.

As he got out of his car he heard a man's voice behind him.

"Sir, you can't park there. I'm going to need you to go around and…"

He never got out his final words as Giovanni turned into him with the knife and drove it high up into his rib cage.

"There. That's it, just let it happen naturally."

The man was trying to suck in air but he failed and his body went limp. Giovanni dragged his body over to a dumpster, lifted the lid and heaved him inside. He cocked his head from side to side to loosen up his muscles and then pressed on towards the entrance. There was only one cruiser outside. Possibly two cops, he figured.

Entering the hospital, he found it was busy dealing with several people who were bleeding. Doctors were yelling orders while nurses scurried around like mice tending to the afflicted. Giovanni didn't go to the front desk to ask. He entered an elevator and went up to the second floor. There he walked along until he saw a sign for staff only. He entered the room and a nurse was eating a sandwich while reading a book. She glanced up briefly but before she could say anything, he sliced her throat. He went back to the door that had a small rectangular window above the handle. He peered out to check that no one was coming. He locked the door and went over to the lockers and began rooting around for scrubs that would fit him. A few minutes later he reappeared in the hallway dressed in scrubs and pushing a trolley full of dirty laundry. It stunk badly. He peered inside and saw sheets with shit on them.

Continuing down past multiple rooms, he peered inside each of them hoping to see her. With five floors, this was going to take some time. He rolled the cart down to the circular desk that was manned by three nurses typing ay keyboards, answering phones and handing off charts to doctors. He pretended to look busy gathering blue plastic bags full of garbage and tossing them into the trolley. He circled the perimeter and watched as they each walked away from the station to help patients. The one that remained didn't look like she was going to budge so Giovanni approached her.

"There's a woman down in room 210 that's asking for help."

"Why hasn't she buzzed?"

"It's not working. Just thought I would let you know."

She nodded, her eyes narrowed slightly and for a moment he thought she might recognize him. Had the staff been given a composite of him? Had they been told to look out for him? Impossible. He'd seen video footage in hospitals before. It was grainy at best. He continued on to the next garbage can, keeping one eye on the nurse. A few minutes and she screeched her chair backwards, letting out a heavy sigh as if annoyed by the fact that she'd have to move her fat ass any further than a few feet from her desk. Once she disappeared out of view he slipped behind the counter and went over to a computer.

It didn't take him long to tap in Theresa Rizzo's name. They had moved her to the fifth floor and placed her in room 508.

"Hey!" one of the nurses returned as he was closing down the window he had opened. "What are you doing?"

He reached for an empty lunch container that was on the counter. He held it up. "Just getting the garbage."

"Okay, well, you're not meant to be in here. Go on now."

She spoke to him like an imbecile. He was tempted to slit her throat where she stood. Instead he walked away and continued pushing the cart down the hallway until he got to the elevator.

The elevator opened and he stepped inside. He pressed the button for the fifth floor. Just as the doors were closing he heard someone call out, "Hold the elevator." A hand slipped through the crack and he found himself looking at a police officer. He kept his eyes focused on the floor as the officer stepped in and turned his back.

"Rough weather out there, eh?" the officer said trying

to make small talk. Giovanni didn't reply. The guy turned and looked at him.

"Don't I know you from somewhere?"

Giovanni shook his head and continued to look down. Behind his back he reached for the knife. His fingers wrapped tightly around it preparing to withdraw. The elevator dinged and the officer smiled and walked out. When the doors slid closed, he relaxed his grip and remained poised as the elevator went up to the next floor.

Chapter 33

Two helicopters zipped overhead. With the torrential rain making the mud feel like quicksand, every step was harder than the next. It wouldn't take them long to know that one of their own was missing. No doubt the reason they had shown up was because of Billy and him. He had no idea what had happened to Billy. More than likely he was dead.

Agent Baker was still out cold. With both of them soaked to the bone, she was beginning to weigh a ton. He had to cut her loose but without a key, the next best thing would be a hair clip or something with a flat edge that could be jammed between the teeth. It was a common method of getting out of cuffs. They were miles from a hospital. If he didn't get her wound looked at soon, she was going to die from loss of blood. Her face had turned pale in color.

As he broke out of the tree line on to a main road, he

had no idea where he was. Vehicles rushed by splashing up water. His body trembled from the cold. As he walked along the side of the road carrying her, a car pulled up and a woman opened her door.

"Is she okay?" she yelled out.

The handcuffs were out of view. All she would have seen was Jack carrying Isabel in his arms.

"She's had a fall in the woods. I need to get her to a hospital."

"There's isn't one close by. The nearest thing is a veterinary clinic."

Jack came up to the car and asked the woman to open the back door. She looked hesitant.

"She's lost a lot of blood, lady. If you don't help us she is going to die."

She opened the door and Jack slipped into the back with Agent Baker in his arms. The woman pulled away off the hard shoulder and glanced back in her mirror. Jack locked eyes with her and looked back down at Agent Baker.

"What happened?"

Jack didn't reply. He didn't want to have to come up with some excuse. Nothing he said would have made the woman believe him. Right now he just wanted to get help. The car swerved a little and the woman apologized.

"The roads are as slick as ice." She had her windshield wipers on full blast and Jack still couldn't see clearly out the window. Everything was a blur of movement. A silhouette of cars rushing by and then disappearing within a matter of seconds.

"How much further?"

"Just over the rise."

As the car bumped its way forward, Jack could feel the agent's heartbeat, she murmured a little and then went silent. He kept checking to make sure she hadn't died. The vehicle pulled into a small parking lot out the front of a wooden shack that had an image of pets on the outside. It wasn't ideal but it would have to do. The woman came out and Jack heaved himself and Agent Baker out of the car. She opened the door to the building and he entered.

From the moment he was inside, a look of shock spread across the faces of two young girls who were manning the front desk. There was no one in there besides them.

"I need to see a doctor."

"This is not a hospital."

Jack laid her down on one of the leather couches they had for visitors, then pulled the Glock and aimed it at them. "Do as I say." Both of them threw their hands up and one of them rushed out back. Barely able to hold the gun in his cuffed hand, he instructed the other girl to lock the door and then head out back. She did as she was told. She was shaking. He didn't like this one bit but he had no choice.

He picked up Agent Baker again and shuffled into the back room. A female veterinarian looked as shocked as her two assistants as Jack laid out Isabel on a table. All the while he kept the gun on them.

"Do you have a hairpin, or something thin and flat?"

One of the assistants pulled one from her hair and nervously handed it to him. There were several ways to do it. One was to jam it into the keyhole, pivot and the ratchet mechanism that pushed against the teeth would come loose. The other was to slide a thin piece of metal between the teeth. It didn't take him long to get loose.

"Now patch her up."

"I'm not trained for this."

"Just do what you can until we can get an ambulance here."

She reached for a few bandages, and ripped open the agent's shirt. She then told one of the girls to phone for an ambulance. The girl was about to go when Jack stopped her. "No, you do it from here." He pulled out his cell and handed it to her. She made the call and then handed it back.

"You think she's going to be okay?" Jack asked trying to see the wound.

"I don't know. It's hard to tell. There's a lot of blood. She needs to be at the hospital."

Jack knew he only had ten minutes, tops, before an ambulance showed up and no doubt police would be with them. He'd been in sticky situations like this before but it was different back in New York. He had places to go. He could lay low and hide until it all blew over. But this, this was way over his head. He was in foreign territory. His daughter was still missing. He had police searching for him. This would never blow over. He had just put a target on his back in more ways than one. His only choice now was to get the hell out of there. To leave the city and never return.

"I need keys to one of your vehicles."

"I..."

"Keys. Now!"

One of the younger girls tossed him her keys.

"It's a blue Pontiac, in the back. Tires are not that great."

Tires were the least of his concerns. He backed out with his gun still on them and then disappeared out the rear exit.

Chapter 34

On the fifth floor, Giovanni rolled the trolley forward towards room 508. Outside, seated on a chair was a police officer. He was flipping through his phone and stabbing it with his index finger. He looked up briefly then returned to checking email. Giovanni collected some of the garbage from a nearby room and tossed it in the blue bag in front of him before approaching room 508.

"This room's off limits."

"You think you can get the garbage?"

The officer rolled his eyes, cast a glance down the corridor and entered. Giovanni saw Theresa lying in bed with her eyes closed. He followed the officer in, making sure he was out of sight before he stuck the knife in the side of his neck. The officer flopped back choking on his own blood. Giovanni pulled the knife out and stabbed him again on the floor until he wasn't moving. He glanced up and the woman in the bed wasn't even aware of what had just happened. He moved to the door and checked the corridor before closing it and pulling the blinds.

Moving over to the bed he placed a hand tight over her mouth. Her eyes fluttered open and bulged.

"Do as I say and you will live. Do you understand?"

She mumbled and nodded. "Now I'm going to take my hand off your mouth. You scream and—"

Slowly he removed his hand. He could see the fear in her eyes. He kept one of the guns on her and the other facing towards the door.

"I need you to get in contact with Jack Winchester and don't say you don't have a number. Can you do that?"

She nodded. He handed her his phone and she dialed in the number. Giovanni kept glancing back at the door. He fully expected someone to come in. Whether that was a doctor, nurse or another cop, it was only a matter of time before someone came to check on her.

* * *

Jack was heading south on Interstate 12 when the call

came in. He glanced at his phone and didn't recognize the number. He was about fifteen minutes from New Orleans. He was going to return to his hotel, collect his belongings and leave.

"Jack."

"Theresa?"

The next voice was one he hadn't heard before.

"If you want to see the girl and Theresa alive, come to the East Hospital now. Fifth floor, room 508. Ten minutes."

"Who is this?"

The phone went dead. Jack smacked the steering wheel in frustration. He looked at the clock. With the weather bad and police on the lookout for him, all he needed now was to be forced into speeding. He slammed his foot against the metal and gunned the engine. By now the weather had got even worse. Wind pummeled the side of the car nearly forcing it off the asphalt. He sped past other vehicles, reaching a speed of over ninety miles per hour. He might have made it there in time if it wasn't for a cruiser that pulled in behind him. He heard the sirens before he saw the car. Red and blue lights flashed in his rearview mirror, a blurred image through the torrential downpour.

There was no way he was going to be able to outrun that cruiser in this piece of shit. Besides he couldn't draw more attention to himself than he already had. More than likely they were looking for a blue Pontiac. All he could do was veer off to the side of the road and hope it was just a matter of speed. He'd know within the first few minutes what he was dealing with. He killed the engine and looked in his mirror. The rain blurred his vision of the officer getting out of his cruiser. Jack knew if he stayed in the vehicle he would be asked to show his license and registration, something he couldn't produce.

Jack opened the door and the officer immediately went on the defensive.

"Driver, stay in the vehicle."

Jack put both hands outside showing him that he was unarmed. Of course his Glock was inside his jacket. He didn't want to kill an officer but he sure as hell didn't want his kid to die. He stepped out of the vehicle ignoring the officer's instructions.

"I said stay in the vehicle. Are you deaf?"

He played the deaf card for all it was worth.

"Turn away and get down on your knees."

Jack could hear the officer approaching from behind with his weapon still drawn. He felt the handcuff click around one wrist and then he was pushed down to the ground. The officer placed a knee on his shoulder while he locked the other cuff on him. His radio crackled and the officer patted him down and pulled the Glock.

Within a matter of seconds, he had Jack up against the car but in a seated position.

He listened to the officer radio in an update and ask them to run a check on the license plate. Obviously the veterinarian hadn't told them in all the drama, or perhaps the ambulance hadn't got there yet? Either way. The moment they ran those plates, and he failed to produce a license and registration, they would know immediately that it was stolen.

Sure enough the cop came over and hauled him up. While the officer had been calling it in, Jack had taken out the pin the vet had given him to undo the handcuffs from Agent Baker. He'd squeezed it into the hole and twisted it around. With the officer having placed his gun back in his holster he knew he could take him. Slammed against the side of the police cruiser, the officer went to open the back door when the handcuffs clicked and fell away. What happened next occurred so fast the officer didn't even have a chance to go for his weapon. Jack yanked one arm around the neck of the officer and pulled him to the ground. He wasn't trying to kill him, just choke him out until he went unconscious.

All the while vehicles were zipping past in the rain. He didn't worry about anyone stopping to help. Visibility was so low with the rain that he was surprised that there hadn't been a ten-car pileup by now. The officer's breathing became faint and then he went unconscious. Moving fast, he dragged him over to the Pontiac and placed him in the back, removed his radio and took his gun. He returned to the cruiser, hopped in and gunned it out of there.

By the time the officer woke up, Jack would be at the hospital. He knew the cop was only trying to do his job, and under any other conditions he might have just let him take him. But he had Theresa and Ruby to think about. He glanced at the clock. Ten minutes had already gone by.

"Please be alive," he muttered.

Chapter 35

He'd been staring at the clock for the past ten minutes.

"The weather's bad. You have to give him time," Theresa stammered.

Every few minutes, Giovanni glanced out the window checking for cars coming into the lot, then checked the corridor. He was beginning to feel antsy. He didn't like this one bit. Congealed blood from the officer pooled on the floor at the foot of the bed.

"Phone him again."

Theresa didn't even hesitate. She dialed the number and waited, but this time there was no answer. A cold shot of fear ran through Giovanni. It was the first time that he had felt nervous. He was outside of his country, out of his element and walking a fine line by returning to the very place he had shot up.

"Maybe's he's stuck in traffic or dropped his phone?"

Giovanni moved over to the door and then he saw

him. Not Jack but the officer from the elevator. He was approaching with two coffees in his hands. He didn't look surprised to see his partner not there. Giovanni stood behind the door waiting for him to enter. He raised a finger to his mouth to make sure that Theresa knew if she said anything, it would be the last thing she would say.

"Mac?"

He heard the coffee being placed down and the door open. The officer seemed as if he was in the process of asking where his partner was when he saw the blood on the floor. Giovanni sprang into action and pressed the tip of his gun against the cop's head. He didn't even think twice. He unloaded a round sending brain matter against the window. His body flopped to the floor like a sack of potatoes. Giovanni dragged him over to his partner. Now the floor was covered in blood. Tears streamed down the woman's face as he rolled the one officer on top of the other, then used a towel from the washroom to wipe down the window.

He glanced at the clock on the wall.

"Five minutes. If he's not here —"

"Where's my daughter?" Before he could finish she cut him off.

"She's safe. In a motel nearby."

"Which one?"

He didn't answer her as he continued to go through the same routine of looking out the window, then down the corridor.

* * *

Hurricane Danielle had already caused mass devastation. Outside the wind was reaching epic proportions. Everything and anything that wasn't bolted down was torn apart and lifted in the air. The only upside to it was that few police would be coming out looking for him. All their efforts would be thrown into public safety, which would include their own. Jack veered into the parking lot that was empty of people. There were about two hundred cars. He drove around close to the front doors, shut off the engine and hopped out. From the cruiser he removed the police shotgun. He tucked his

Glock and the officer's piece into the small of his back. Before he went in, he went to the back of the vehicle and took out a large yellow raincoat with a New Orleans Police Department logo sewed onto it. The cop's hat was still in the cruiser. He put that on and slipped the shotgun underneath his jacket as to not cause alarm when entering the main hospital lobby. To anyone looking on, he was nothing more than a cop.

Large droplets of water dropped from the raincoat as he approached the elevator. It dinged and as the doors opened an officer stepped out.

"Oh hey," he glanced at Jack. Jack tipped his hat further and kept his eyes down. "What are you here for?"

"Shift change."

The officer frowned as Jack stepped into the elevator.

"But that doesn't occur for another four hours."

"I was called in early because of the weather."

"By who?"

Jack swallowed. "Look, man, I don't call the shots. I just show up and do the work."

He stared intently. "Are you a new hire?"

Jack hit the button on the elevator for the fifth floor. He cleared his throat. "Yeah."

Before the doors slid closed the cop stepped back inside. "I'll ride up with you. I need to speak to Mac, he's not picking up."

"Probably taking a piss," Jack replied.

"So how's the weather holding up out there?"

"It's not getting any better."

He tried to act normal but he could feel beads of sweat rolling down his back. The last thing he wanted to do was harm a cop. No matter how he saw this go down, he was liable to get hurt. His mind flipped through various scenarios.

"So is this your first shift?"

"Yep."

The officer looked him up and down, then the expression on his face changed as he glanced down at his shoes and pants. His eyes came up to meet Jack's. Jack had already anticipated what he would do next. Before the cop could go for his gun, Jack punched him twice in the face, took out his gun and used the butt of it to knock him unconscious. He slumped down against the side of the elevator. Jack glanced up at the light as it illuminated the floor levels.

He regretted having to knock him out but at least he was alive. He took a moment to handcuff him. He finished up just as the elevator reached the fifth floor. As he stepped out onto the floor, he cast a glance both ways. He saw the numbers on the wall indicating the rooms. Before he made his way to Theresa, he alerted the nurses who were at the desk to get out.

"What?" One of them must have thought he was joking.

"Take the staircase, when you reach the bottom floor, alert the others and get out of the building."

Their eyes widened in horror but they didn't hesitate or question him. All they saw was the police hat and raincoat. That's all anyone saw when they met police. People didn't question the law, especially if their lives were at stake. His heart began pounding in his chest as he kept the Glock low and he passed room 502, 504 and 506. The door to room 508 was closed, the blinds pulled shut. He paused with his back to the wall. There was no easy way to do this. Whoever the guy was, he already had the advantage. If Jack burst in, chances were he would be blown away, or Theresa might be hurt. Then there was the fact that he might not be working alone. Jack looked around. Before he made a decision on what to do he went to each of the rooms and told the occupants to get out if they could walk. They wanted an explanation, he couldn't give them one but showing the Glock got them moving. As the corridor filled up with patients heading for the stairs he returned to room 508.

With his hand on the handle he slowly pushed it down and cracked the door open. He figured he would see Theresa or the barrel of a gun but there was no one inside. He pushed the door wide open, glanced around and then stepped inside. It was empty.

Then, in the reflection of the window he saw him.

"Drop the gun."

Jack released his weapon. It clattered as it hit the floor. The next thing he felt was a whack on the back of his skull, and everything went black.

DEBT COLLECTOR: HARD TO KILL

Chapter 36

The sudden slap of freezing cold water snapped him back into consciousness. Blinking hard, the world came back into view. He found he was in a room that resembled an operating room. Laid out on a gurney, his arms and legs were held down by leather straps.

"Finally awake." The man didn't look at him, he had his back turned. Jack hadn't even seen his face, only the memory of his blurred reflection. Jack's head was throbbing hard at the base of his skull. He glanced down and saw that his shirt had been ripped open.

"Who are you?"

"It doesn't matter."

"Who sent you?"

Not even replying, he turned and wheeled over a steel surgical trolley. Laid out on the top were scalpels, scissors and other various indistinguishable tools. A bright light was shining down on his face. As his eyes adjusted to where he was, he got a sense that he wasn't in surgery but what looked like a basement. The hospital basement? Large rusty pipes and exposed vents snaked their way across the ceiling. The man was a wearing a white shirt, his sleeves rolled up.

"I have to admit, after everything that I'd heard about you, I thought it would have been harder than this."

"Where's my daughter? Where's Theresa?"

"You know, I once had a daughter." He paused holding up a scalpel to his chin, lost in thought. "She was beautiful. I never imagined I could love a person as much as I did her. She was just full of life. I had a wife too."

"What do you want?"

"It's not what I want. Do you remember Vito Nicchi?" he paused. "Of course you do. You killed him."

"You have your facts wrong. I didn't kill him. SWAT did."

He studied Jack's face.

"SWAT. You. It doesn't matter now."

He pulled up a seat and got real close. An Italian with

thick black hair and a chiseled chin stared at Jack, studying him like a lab rat.

"You and I we are cut from the same cloth. We have a job to do. It's not personal. It's business, you understand."

"We're not the same."

"No?"

"I killed those who were responsible for their actions. I didn't kill Vito. Vito's men killed my sister, and my father."

"But you would have, right?"

He tapped Jack's bare chest with the flat side of the scalpel.

"Where's Theresa and my daughter?"

He didn't reply but continued to stare at him. Finally he said, "You know what, Jack. I believe you. You see, men like us, we don't have any reason to lie. If you say you didn't kill Vito, I believe you. However, that doesn't change what needs to happen today."

Jack let out a laugh.

"Something amusing?"

"It's the irony. I spent my whole killing people for money. Those who owed. Those who couldn't pay. Those who needed to pay. Now I'm one of them and I didn't even do it. Ironic right?"

"Death comes to us all."

Jack tugged on the straps but they were tight. There was no getting out of this. Fate seemed to have a strange sense of humor. "What's going to happen to my daughter?"

"What do you think?" He stared back. "What would you do in my shoes, Jack?"

"I wouldn't kill them."

The man ran a hand over his chin. A slight look of amusement danced across his face.

"That's how you justify it, is it?"

"What?"

"What we do. You expect me to believe you've never killed a woman or child?"

"I don't expect you to believe anything. You can go to

hell for all I care."

He smirked. "You know how many people I have killed, Jack?"

Jack rolled his eyes. They were all the same. Egotistical pricks who kept count of how many lives they had taken.

"Let me guess, you have a belt with notches of every life you've taken?"

He tapped Jack and let out a chuckle. "No. I've lost count."

He got up and walked out of the room. Jack heard a scuffle and then Theresa came into view. He was holding her by the back of the neck and forcing her forward. Tears rolled down her cheeks as she stumbled forward and fell to the floor. "Jack."

"Here's what I'm going to do, Jack. I believe you. I really do. For that, I'm going to extend the courtesy that wasn't extended to me when men killed my wife and child. I'll give you a minute to say goodbye."

He grabbed a hold of Theresa by her hair and yanked her up, tossing her against Jack.

"Go on now."

He stepped back and watched as Theresa looked at him.

"Hurry up before I change my mind."

Theresa looked at Jack. "I'm so sorry, Jack."

"It's not your fault. I shouldn't have come here."

Her tears dropped onto his chest.

"Oh this is magic. A real Hallmark moment," the man said from behind. With Theresa blocking the man's view of Jack, he motioned with his eyes to the surgical instruments. Theresa's eyes followed his gaze without moving her head.

"I never understood the men who killed my family, but now I do."

Jack continued to talk to her about his daughter while he gestured with his eyes. There was a slim chance that she'd be able to do anything but they had nothing to lose. This wasn't going to end well for either of them.

"Alright that's enough."

As he dragged Theresa back, Jack watched her grab up

a scalpel. The man led her out of the room. Jack's pulse was racing. Not even ten seconds had passed when he heard a high-pitched scream. The door burst open and Theresa came stumbling in not even looking back for one second. Her hands were covered in blood. She immediately began loosening the strap holding Jack's wrists down. She had managed to get both his hands free when Giovanni came staggering back into the room holding a hand to the side of his neck and wheeling a gun around. He looked disoriented. Theresa ducked down. Bullets ricocheted off steel as he fired at her. She rammed a metal trolley towards him knocking him backwards. The gun flew out of his hand. By now Jack had his legs unstrapped. He leapt off the gurney and lunged at Giovanni who was in the process of getting the gun.

In a struggle for control, the gun went off several times and bullets pinged off the metal. One bullet hit a pipe and it burst open letting out a blast of hot steam. Giovanni kicked Jack off him and fired a round at Theresa. The shot hit her in the leg and she collapsed to the ground. On the ground, Jack reached for the metallic tray that had once held the surgical instruments. He tossed it at Giovanni and then lunged at him again.

By now the once clean floor was bathed in blood from both Giovanni's wound and Theresa's. Slipping on blood, it became even harder to fight as they struggled to stay upright. Jack plowed into him with a right hook, only to feel the full force of a jab in the side of his ribs. The gun Giovanni had been holding was knocked out of his hands again and slid across the ground. As he went to retrieve it, Jack drove into him full force and they fell back though the double doors. Beaten back, Giovanni managed to get on top of Jack. With his hands around his throat he tried to choke him. Jack drove a knee up into his groin, reached up and dug his thumbs into Giovanni's eyes. He let out an excruciating scream and released his grip. Jack pushed him off, took a hold of him by the scruff of his neck and dragged him back into the room. Steam poured out of a pipe as Jack tried to force him into it. Giovanni grabbed his leg and bit deep into it. Jack screamed in agony and fell back. Standing to his feet, Giovanni grabbed up what looked like a bone cutter off a counter. He lifted it in his hands as Jack writhed around on the floor in agony.

Right then the sound of a gun going off three times resounded. The echo was so loud it was almost deafening. Giovanni gripped his stomach, blood trickled over his fingers as he dropped to his knees. Behind him on the floor sat Theresa with both arms outstretched and the gun in her hands.

Jack, gripping his leg, slid over to Theresa. She just held the gun. Her eyes wide. Her skin pale with shock. Slowly Jack removed the gun from her grip and pulled her into his arms.

"It's okay, it's over."

Her hands were shaking. Her body was stiff as he held her tightly and glanced back at the assailant.

"Come on, let's get you out of here."

Jack rose to his feet helping her up with one arm around her. They staggered slowly towards the door. As he pushed the door open to leave, he heard a sound behind him.

"Jack."

Jack wheeled around with the gun just as Giovanni came at him. He fired two shots into him, and he collapsed to the floor. Both of them stared down at the lifeless body before staggering away.

Chapter 37

Jack awoke from his slumber. He'd hitched a ride with a local trucker who was heading south. He had no destination in mind. All that mattered was getting as far away as possible. He'd learned firsthand what Eddie had warned him about. He couldn't be around anyone who he cared for. It was too dangerous. It wasn't just the FBI that was after him but others would come. A debt was never forgiven. In the criminal underworld only blood could atone for wrongs committed.

The following two weeks, Jack continued to hitch rides, sleep in cheap motels and stay on the move. He figured if he didn't stay too long in one place, the chances of him being found were slim.

Three weeks after the night at the hospital in New Orleans, Jack placed a phone call to Theresa. It hadn't taken the police long to find Ruby. Forty-eight hours later she had been reunited with her mother. As Giovanni hadn't mentioned the name of the motel, they had to contact every motel in a twenty-mile radius. Safe but shaken up by the whole ordeal, she was placed into care until Theresa was well enough to get out of the hospital. Kalen's arrest had led to the apprehension of Tex and now both of them were staring down a lengthy sentence.

"Have you heard any more from Agent Baker?" Jack asked.

"She came by in the first week. She had a whole bunch of questions, told me if I heard from you to let her know."

"How did she look?"

"She made a remark about you saving her life?"

Jack chuckled a little.

"And, she said that perhaps she had misjudged you. But that didn't change anything. She was still going to bring you in."

"I wouldn't expect any less."

"Though, you'll be pleased to know your mug shot isn't being shown on any Amber Alerts."

There was a pause.

"How is she?"

"She doing okay, Jack."

Jack didn't say anything further. There was very little he could say. News that he had a daughter had been shocking enough. Not being able to stay was the hardest thing he had to do. But it was for the best.

"What about Billy?"

"He didn't make it."

"Sorry."

"I think we would have gone our separate ways eventually."

"Yeah, maybe."

Theresa didn't ask him if she would see him again. She knew him better than anyone else. Danger followed him. His life wasn't ever going to be ordinary, even if that was what he wanted now.

"You going to be okay?" Jack asked.

"You know me, Jack. I bounce back."

"Yeah, you do."

She took a deep breath. "I've been in contact with my sister in San Francisco, so we're going to move in with her."

"That's a good idea."

She was a strong woman. Like Jack, her upbringing had been hard. It had shaped who she was today. He had no doubt that she would eventually find someone good for her. Someone good for Ruby. Someone who could give them a life with all the little things that mattered. All the things he only wished he could give.

"They'll be keeping tabs on you," Jack said.

"I wouldn't be surprised if they are listening to this."

"Yeah." He paused. "Well, take care of yourself, Theresa, and Ruby."

"Will do."

The line went dead and Jack felt a deep ache inside. Before he tossed the disposable phone, he pulled out a piece of paper he'd taken from Agent Baker's room. The one with Dana's name, number and address. He dialed the number and waited, looking out at the trucks in the service station.

The phone was answered. "Hello?"

It was Dana Grant.

"Hello?"

Jack didn't answer. He hung up, tossed the phone into a garbage can, slung his bag over his shoulder and dashed across the small road to the line of Mack Trucks.

"Can I get a ride?"

"Where you heading?"

"I haven't decided yet."

With that, he stepped up into to the truck and slammed the door. The truck roared to life and eased out of the truck stop. A light rain began to fall and as he stared out the window he thought about what lay ahead.

There was no telling what tomorrow would bring.

He didn't know what the next town would offer or whose path he would cross.

Every day was another chance to start again.

One day. One hour. One minute at a time.

That's how he would live his life.

* * *

THANK YOU FOR READING

Now read Book 5 Angel of Death

Please take a second to leave a review, it's really

appreciated. Thanks kindly, Jon.

Newsletter

Thank you for buying Debt Collector 4:Hard to Kill

Building a relationship with readers is one of the best things about writing. I occasionally send out a newsletter with details on new releases and subscriber only special offers. For instance, with each new release of a book, you will be alerted to it at a subscriber only discounted rate.

Go here to receive special offers, bonus content, and news about Jon's new books, sign up for the newsletter. http://www.jonmills.com/

A Plea...

If you enjoyed the book, I would really appreciate it if you would consider leaving a review. I can't stress how helpful this is in helping other readers decide if they should give it a shot. Reviews from readers like you are the best recommendation a book can have. Without reviews, an author's books are virtually invisible on the retail sites. It also lets me know what you liked. You can leave a review by visiting the book's page. I would greatly appreciate it. It only takes a couple of seconds.

Thank you — **Jon Mills**

ABOUT THE AUTHOR

Jon Mills is originally from England. He currently lives in Ontario, Canada with his family. He is the author of The Debt Collector series, Lost Girls, I'm Still Here, The Promise, True Connection, and the Undisclosed Trilogy. He also writes under other pen names. To get more information about upcoming books or if you wish to get in touch with Jon, you can do so using the following contact information:

Twitter: Jon_Mills

Facebook: authorjonmills

Website: www.jonmills.com

Email: contact@jonmills.com

CPSIA information can be obtained
at www.ICGtesting.com
Printed in the USA
FSHW011716010520
69834FS